Kiss Me Not

"No," she whispered, but despite herself, reached up to meet his kiss.

For a long moment they stood, molded against one another, savoring the sweetness of the caress. Then she placed both hands against his chest and attempted to push herself away from him.

"No," she said breathlessly. "This is wrong. We must not!"

Alan felt a deep sense of loss as she moved away from him. "You are right," he reluctantly agreed. "I ought not to have done that—even though I have been longing to do so for many days."

"*We* ought not," her voice trembled; it was taking all her strength not to return to his arms. "For I did nothing to stop you. Rather, I encouraged you. And it was more wrong for me than it was for you. After all, I must not forget that I am a married woman."

Diamond Books by Monette Cummings

A HUSBAND FOR HOLLY
SCARLET LADY
A KISS FOR CAROLINE

A Kiss For Caroline

MONETTE CUMMINGS

DIAMOND BOOKS, NEW YORK

A KISS FOR CAROLINE

A Diamond Book / published by arrangement with
the author

PRINTING HISTORY
Diamond edition / June 1991

ISBN: 1-55773-527-1

Diamond Books are published by The Berkley Publishing
Group, 200 Madison Avenue, New York, New York 10016.
The name "DIAMOND" and its logo are trademarks
belonging to Charter Communications, Inc.

PRINTED IN THE UNITED STATES OF AMERICA

10 9 8 7 6 5 4 3 2 1

Prologue

How her head ached. It seemed to her that there were heavy weights of some kind pressing powerfully upon her eyes, holding them closed. Would it be worth the effort it would take to open them? Perhaps if she could sleep again . . .

It was of no use. The throbbing in her head had become so fierce that it banished any chance of further sleep. When she put up a hand, she could feel a cloth of some sort about her head and a spot which was painful to her touch. She forced her eyes to open, wondering where she was.

She was lying on a narrow bed. Her neck was so stiff she dared not turn her head to look about, but she did not think she had ever been on this type of bed before.

A face bent over her, that of a plainly dressed young woman she did not recall having seen before. "You are awake at last," the woman said, smiling. "That is good. I must tell my father."

The young woman was gone before she could speak, but soon returned, followed by a tall, gray-haired man. He seemed to be another stranger. He put his warm fingers

1

against her wrist and looked into her eyes. "How do you feel today?" he asked.

She tried to shake her head, but the pain was so great that she was forced to close her eyes again for a moment, until the nausea had passed. She licked her dry lips in an effort to make speaking easier. The young woman quickly brought over a glass of water and, raising her head slightly, held the glass to her lips so she might swallow deeply. Then she said her first word. "Caroline?" she asked.

"No, this is Helen. And I am Doctor Ward. Who is Caroline?"

"I—I do not know. But she—" She could barely manage to get out the next words. "Fi– find Caroline."

"We shall find her for you. You must not worry about her. It is not good for you," the doctor said in soothing tones, while his daughter stroked her brow, careful not to touch the bandage on one temple. "Now tell us, what is your name?"

Her eyes flew open. Brown eyes looked up in bewilderment.

"I—" she pressed a hand to her head and winced as she touched the wound. "I do not know. Can you not tell me? Who am I and why am I here?"

Chapter One

Since entering this neighborhood of mean, litter-filled streets, the gleaming black carriage with its handwrought silver trim and its team of matched black horses had been followed by increasing crowds of curious folk. Most were dirty, ragged children, but some of their equally dirty elders—at least those who were not too gin-soaked or who had not been otherwise occupied picking pockets and the like—also trailed after the carriage.

When it halted, the crowd drew closer, all eager to see what sort of person occupied so grand an equipage. Several were hoping there might be something which could be picked up by clever fingers. A number of these fingers were already touching the silver trimmings, to see how much force it would take to wrench them off the coach.

Fully aware of their intentions, the coachman leaped to the ground and waved his whip about him threateningly to drive them off. "Out of my sight, you filthy dogs!"

The onlookers moved back, gaping as the coachman opened the door and announced doubtfully, "This is the place you said you wished to come, Miss Ainsworth."

"Lower the steps, then, fool," his passenger ordered sharply, "and let me down."

"But—" He looked about him at the street, more like a rubbish heap than a thoroughfare, and at the ragged people who stood about staring.

If he left the carriage even for the time it would take him to accompany the lady to the door, the vehicle would be stripped of its silver trim, its fittings, doubtless even its horses before his return. Still, could he allow her to go even a few steps unaccompanied—to trust that she would not be accosted or robbed? "This is no fit place for a lady such as you to be calling."

"I shall be the judge of that." The tone was more peremptory than before. "You will wait for me."

The man considered another protest, then shrugged and lowered the steps, swinging quickly about to protect his carriage from any who might dare to come too near it. His passenger's haughty glance was enough to quell any watchers who might have been tempted to approach her. She ignored their comments as she picked her way between the mounds of filth to the steps of the building.

At least the steps, she noted, showed signs of having been scrubbed a short time ago and, despite a great number of footprints which doubtless had been made more recently, were far cleaner and lacking in debris than those which led to the neighboring buildings. Miss Ainsworth merely sniffed at this indication of neatness in so foul an area as this, and rapped the knocker soundly upon the white door.

Everything about the lady, from the expensive tailoring of her fur-trimmed black pelisse and the gown which could be glimpsed beneath it, to the equally expensive veiling that fell from her feather-topped bonnet to hide her face, spelled Quality. Helen Ward, who opened the door, took the opportunity to peer quickly into the street to see if the carriage bore a crest.

Most wealthy Londoners probably had no idea that such a squalid part of the city existed. Nor, if they had known about it, would they have cared a tittle. Anything beyond the narrow confines of their own gas-lit streets might well have been in some foreign land for all the interest it evoked in them. The only exception to their insularity was the road which led them to Brighton, and that thoroughfare was rescued from oblivion only when the Prince Regent had removed to his summer residence.

Even through the veiling, Helen noticed condescension with which the lady scrutinized the well-worn rug in the hallway, and the faded and scarred furnishings visible through an open doorway.

"Do you call *this* a hospital?" There was deep criticism in her tone.

The girl resented this slur upon her surroundings, which she knew were little more than beggarly. How could they be otherwise, when most of their patients had no money even to pay for the treatment her father gave them gladly? However, she was much too well bred to answer in kind. "No, Madam, this is the residence and surgery of Doctor Ward. He is my father. Did you wish to see him?"

"But you do keep patients here?"

"Sometimes we do so. If you will come in, I shall call my father. He makes all such arrangements."

"I understand that you are keeping a young person here who does not remember her name," the other persisted, bristling at the suggestion that *she* might be the sort who wished to enter a doctor's care in this area of town. "Is that correct?"

"Please—you must speak to my father about these things." Helen did not consider it the right thing for her to discuss her father's work—and especially not with this censorious lady.

"Very well—if you cannot or will not tell me what I wish to know, perhaps he will have the intelligence to do so."

At this last slur, she stepped back without another word to allow the other to enter the house, then closed the outer door and walked swiftly away, leaving the caller standing in the dim hallway. Normally, Helen would have ushered even the most ragged man or woman into the small room which served as the family parlor as well as a waiting room for her father's patients. But this lady, who was so scornful of everything about her, did not deserve, she felt, to be so treated and, despite her training, she found it impossible to continue being polite to her.

She tapped softly at a door at the far end of the hall. "Father," she said. "There is a caller to see you."

Although these were not supposed to be his surgery hours, such calls upon his service were commonplace in this rough neighborhood, so the doctor replied at once. He came to meet the visitor, directing a frown at his daughter as he passed her.

"Why did you not bring the lady into the parlor, Helen?" he asked, but his daughter shrugged and turned away without answering.

He soon had the answer to his daughter's actions. He could see the lady's nose wrinkled discernibly in disgust at the unmistakable odor of disinfectant which surrounded the doctor, an odor to which he and Helen were so accustomed that they paid no attention to it. Most of their neighbors would have been unable to notice it above the reek of their normal surroundings.

The doctor had inherited a small competence, but it was eaten up in his efforts to provide his needy patients with the best of care. Despite the pitiful indigence of the neighborhood in which he worked, Dr. Ward attempted to keep up to date on the medical procedures of the day, which was more than a great number of the more affluent practitioners of the city were in the habit of doing.

The bloodstained coat some physicians preferred to wear as an advertisement of their medical skill was not for him. His surgery was kept spotless, and he fought daily in a vain attempt to have the wards he visited treated in the same manner. Cleanliness in all regards for his patients was important to him; he felt it might save lives which would otherwise have been lost.

He now understood why Helen had treated this expensively dressed woman so discourteously. For all the thoughtfulness she showed to his patients, Helen was perhaps over-proud of their humble surroundings and of his work. She would not take kindly to any slur upon it.

"I understand you wished to consult me, Madam," he said. Since the caller had not raised her veil, he supposed she intended to remain anonymous, and that this would prove to be the sort of matter on which she would not care to consult her family physician. A lady of Quality who found herself in a difficult position customarily preferred to consult someone who did not know her and could not gossip about her. None of the doctors with whom he was familiar were prone to gossip, but a lady would doubtless prefer not to take a chance.

He stifled a sigh. Such procedures were abhorrent to him and, although he felt that she would be well able to pay for his services, he knew he must decline to help her. "Will you step into my surgery, and we shall see what we can do about your problem?"

"My only problem," her voice had sharpened, as if she were unaccustomed to being denied immediate obedience to her slightest wish, "is that no one here appears to be able to answer a simple question. I asked if you had a young person here who does not know who she is."

"May I ask your reason for wishing to know about her, Madam?" He was relieved to learn that he was wrong about her reason for coming to him, but he was determined to protect his patient. "We have had a number of curiosity seekers calling here and asking to see her in the past several days, but I should not think that you are that type of person."

The caller threw back her veil, revealing a face that had undoubtedly been considered pretty in her youth. Now that she had reached what the doctor judged to be an age somewhere beyond her thirtieth year, her face had taken on a certain sharpness.

Nonetheless, he owned that she was still an attractive female. Her outstanding features were her eyes. They were a clear green, and the force of her gaze was so intense that even the doctor, accustomed as he was to dealing with people of all sorts, found himself impressed by its power.

"I am Miss Ainsworth." Her tone was crisp, as if she considered any explanation of her motives unnecessary, that she considered such questions verged on the impertinent.

"I assure you, doctor, that it is not mere curiosity which brings me here. I consider emotions of that sort to be most ill-bred. There was, however, an item in the local newspaper about this young person."

"Yes. Normally, I have to deplore the tendency of the newspapers to print such items, as they frequently are the cause of much unhappiness, either to the patient or to her family, by leading members of the public to read into them some hint of wrongdoing. Some people are far too prone to do so. In this case, however, I hoped that the publicity would bring forward someone who could tell me who the young lady might be."

"The item described her as a lady, as do you," she said. "Can you tell me how it happens that she is a patient in your care?" Her voice implied that no true lady would be in this place. The doctor chose to ignore the slur upon his surroundings.

"Certainly. She was badly injured when the stagecoach in which she was riding overturned—due, I have been given to understand, to the fact that a young gentleman who had imbibed more than was good for him had forcibly taken the lines from the regular driver, but was unable to control the team. Unfortunately, this sort of thing happens much too often, and often with results even more tragic than in this young lady's case."

The visitor's frown reminded him that he was straying toward a issue which was of great importance to him, but doubtless would hold no interest for a lady who might never need to set foot in a stagecoach. He hastened to continue, "The young lady was thrown from the coach when it fell— I believe she must have been riding in one of the cheaper seats on the roof—and was struck on the head, causing her loss of memory."

"I have heard that such things may occur as a result of such an injury, but have wondered if there was any truth to the tale."

"Unlike many rumors one may hear about illnesses, most of which are unfounded, there is a great deal of truth to the one about such matters—unfortunately, as happened in this case. The young lady was brought to me, without any sort of identification and, since regaining consciousness, has been unable to tell us anything about herself."

Her gaze grew sharper. "That is most unusual, is it not, even in the case of an impecunious person. I mean, any person who travels would certainly carry some means of identifying herself, would she not?"

"Doubtless, she would have had such things when she set out upon her journey, but they were lost or stolen while she was unconscious. And apparently no one upon the coach had the opportunity—or the interest—to learn anything about her. I have several small rooms at the back of the house which I use from time to time for patients who have nowhere to go—which often happens in this neighborhood. Since I hesitated to send the young lady to a hospital, where she almost certainly would have been considered mad, I have kept her here, hoping to be able to find her family."

Miss Ainsworth nodded. "And that is why I have come to see her. I must tell you, painful as the subject is to us, that my brother's wife has gone missing and that we have been searching for her for several days."

"I see. And you think—"

The visitor, it appeared, would not take kindly to any attempt on the part of another to dominate the conversation. "Edward Ainsworth, my brother, is at present in the north, following a rumor that his wife might have been seen in that area. When the story of your patient was brought to my attention, I thought it might be possible—however unlikely—that my sister-in-law had come as far away from her home as this. Therefore, I should like to ascertain for myself whether your 'mystery woman,' as the newspaper has called her, might be the one we seek."

"Since that is the case, Miss Ainsworth, I certainly have no objection to your seeing the young lady. If she is your sister-in-law, your presence might be enough to revive her memory."

"I trust you may be right," the visitor said fervently. "Her plight must be a miserable one."

"It is an unhappy state for the child, of course, and one which I am most anxious to relieve."

"Child?" She echoed his word sharply. "I understood you to say that—"

"Oh, she is actually a young lady, one who is nearing her twentieth year, I should suppose, but I have come to think of her as a child. Partially because of her small size, but more because of her deep confusion. You must be warned before you see her that, as a result of the violence of the blow, there is a possibility that she will *not* be able to recognize you."

Again Miss Ainsworth nodded in acceptance, and permitted the doctor to lead the way to a tiny room which was barely large enough to hold a bed and a small table. He placed himself between the lady and the bed and though she tried to pass him, she was only able to catch a glimpse of the patient. As he had said, she appeared to be a very small person. A large bandage covered part of her head; on the side which was uninjured, fair hair escaped from its confinement and spread across the pillow.

First checking the girl's pulse and listening to her even breathing, the doctor at last touched her lightly on the shoulder. Her eyes opened and she smiled as she recognized him.

"Have you found Caroline?" she asked, as she always did upon awakening.

"Not yet, my dear. Unless—" He turned toward the visitor. "Perhaps your name is Caroline?"

"No, and I cannot recall anyone of that name among my sister-in-law's friends."

"Still, I have told you that you must not fret about the matter, young lady," he said to his patient. "It is not good for you to worry about this, or anything else. We shall find her for you before much longer. Now, I have brought you a visitor." He stepped back and allowed Miss Ainsworth to approach the bed.

"April," she said in a coaxing tone. "Do you know me? Say that you do."

The patient's gaze passed slowly over the face bent above her. Then, with a puzzled look in her brown eyes, she shook her head slightly.

"No—I am sorry, but I do not think I have ever seen you. Who are you?"

At the denial, the older lady's face puckered as if she might weep. "Oh, April, please, you must not say that. I am Beatrix. Surely, you must remember."

"Beatrix? Do I know a Beatrix?"

Chapter Two

The stupid, whey-faced chit, the caller said to herself, keeping an expression of deep concern upon her face with an effort. *If she only knew the great amount of trouble I have had. . . . She would be well-served if I were to claim that I had made an error when I first saw her, that I only realized when I spoke to her that she was not April, after all, but merely someone who has a slight resemblance to her. If I were to walk out of this place this instant and leave her to fend for herself, I should do so in a moment . . . if only Edward did not need her so badly. He would not forgive me if he learned I had failed him in something so important as this.*

She struggled to bring her feelings under control and was even able to manage a encouraging smile. "But of course, you must remember me, April dear. I am Beatrix— Edward's sister."

"Who is Edward?"

"Edward, if you knew to what lengths I am going on your account," Beatrix Ainsworth said beneath her breath while she cast an unhappy look at the doctor. "You heard what she said, did you not?" she asked him. "Can it be that she has forgot us all?—her family—everything?"

Touched by the unhappiness the lady displayed, he nodded. "It would appear that is what she has done, Miss Ainsworth. But you ought not to allow yourself to worry overmuch about her present condition. As I told you, this complete loss of memory is something that frequently happens in cases of a head injury. In your sister-in-law's case, it will prove to be merely a temporary state. Or so we shall hope."

"Oh, yes, we must hope that you will be proven right." Miss Ainsworth caught the girl's hand in both of hers, resisting an urge to crush it in her grasp until the girl screamed in pain.

From the first time she had heard of it, she had found the idea of Edward's marriage almost more than she could bear, and the only feeling she had for his young wife was one of the deepest hatred. If things could only be as they had been before. . . . It would not serve, however, for her to do anything at this moment which might cause the doctor to think that she would not be a good guardian for his patient.

"Edward, my dear," she began, making her voice as soft as she could. "Your husband, my brother. You must say that you remember him, dear April."

"I am sorry—"

"It was very naughty of you, dear, to go off as you did, without leaving any word for us, and Edward and I have been quite worried about what might have happened to you. We could not understand where you might have gone or why you had done so."

Fearing his patient might become overset, the doctor touched Miss Ainsworth on the arm, and her tone changed at once.

"But all of that does not matter," she said soothingly, "Not in the least, now that you have been found. I shall send word to Edward at once that you are here in London, and he will hasten to you." Turning to Dr. Ward she said, "Now, doctor, I do not suppose there is a reason why I cannot take my sister-in-law home with me immediately. Her husband will be so happy to see her again—as am I."

Despite her few words of criticism at the first, it was obvious the lady deeply cared for the welfare of his patient. Dr. Ward was unhappy not to be able to please her. However, he could not see that there was any way he could grant her request. "I believe, Miss Ainsworth, it might be the wisest thing for me to have a discussion with your brother before I release his wife to him."

There was a flash of anger in the green eyes. It vanished almost before the doctor could be certain he had seen it, however, and she summoned her most winning smile. It was most important, she had recalled, for her to convince him that her only thought was for the good of his patient, and that any impatience on her part was merely a wish to see that all was well with the younger lady.

"Of course, doctor; I can comprehend the reason for your feeling as you do about the matter. You cannot permit just anyone to come to you, claiming to know your patient, and wishing to take her away. Although I cannot understand why anyone should wish to do so."

"My dear Miss Ainsworth, I fear that I did not make myself entirely clear—"

"I hope you do not think," she shot him a sharp glance, "that *I* could be one of those females who wish to take young girls for—for immoral purposes?"

The doctor reddened. Accustomed as he had become to hearing even rougher language than this from the females of the area, he was deeply shocked by the thought that a lady of her position should know and acknowledge such women existed.

"No—no—my dear lady, I assure you, I had no such thought. No one could possibly think . . . It is only that I feel I should discuss her condition with Mr. Ainsworth before she leaves my care."

The lady smiled at him once more, her earlier anger apparently gone so quickly that it might never have existed. Dr. Ward thought her moods the most changeable of anyone he had known. He hoped her volatility would not bode ill for his patient.

"You are right to feel so strongly about your patient as

you do, of course," she was saying. "If you did not do so, I confess that I should be loath to leave her with you. I shall insist that my brother return home as quickly as may be, and he will come to you." To the girl she said, "You must not fret about being here, April dear."

"Oh, I do not—" She wanted to say that she was not unhappy here, but was not permitted to say as much before the other lady rushed ahead.

"We shall have you away from here just as soon as Edward arrives. And once you are in your own home, you must improve at once. Is that not true, doctor?"

Once more, she appeared to be willing him to agree with her. Much as he would have wished, however, to tell her that she was right, the doctor could not allow himself to hold out hopes which might prove false and cause the family great disappointment.

"One can make no positive statements about cases such as this, Miss Ainsworth, for each is different. Frequently, it seems to be an excellent thing for a person who is suffering as is your sister-in-law—I do not speak of actual pain, for that will soon disappear, but rather of her mental anguish— to see familiar objects and hear familiar voices. The memory is quite unpredictable; it can stirred by almost anything."

"Then I shall send my brother to you as soon as he comes home. The sooner we can take my sister-in-law into surroundings she knows, the better it will be for her, I am certain."

She cast a disparaging look about the tiny room, then drew the heavy veil over her face once more and walked out. The doctor's daughter, who had been waiting in the hall, hurried ahead to open the door for her. When she was gone, Helen swept the hall carpet vigorously, as if she hoped to remove any sign of the visitor who had scorned her father's surgery. Telling himself that such a display of her feelings was quite understandable in one as young as Helen, and was certainly harmless, the doctor smiled at her and returned to the patient's room.

"That was not Caroline, was it?" she asked, her tone anxious.

"No, my dear. She said that her name was Beatrix. Do you not remember?"

"Oh yes—Beatrix." She wrinkled her brow in an effort to find a place in her non-existent memory for something about the caller but, as always, there was nothing for her to find. The lady who had said that she was Beatrix had appeared to be quite solicitous of her, but . . .

"I do not believe that she likes me."

"Now, young lady," the doctor said bracingly, "you must not begin to imagine things merely because you cannot yet place the lady in your memory. Unhappy thoughts of that kind are not good for you and can only delay your recovery."

"It only seems—"

"After all, she is your husband's sister—certainly, she must be fond of you. Did she not come here hoping that she might find you and tell us how worried she and her brother had been for your safety? I can assure you, my dear, that coming to this neighborhood would not be a pleasant journey for a lady."

"Ye-es, I suppose you are right."

She did not sound as if she had been convinced by his argument, and he spoke more forcefully. "You must believe me, my child. I know I am right about her deep concern for you. The lady was most eager to take you home at once. Doubtless, any anger she might have felt was directed at me because I would not allow you to leave here until your husband comes."

To himself, Dr. Ward said that his patient might be correct in her feelings about her sister-in-law. It was common for a spinster who had reached her middle thirties—as he had judged Miss Ainsworth to have done—to be jealous of anyone whom her brother had wed, especially a bride who was fifteen or sixteen years younger than she, and far prettier. At least, the doctor found the younger lady more attractive. And probably, the husband's eyes did too. No doubt Miss Ainsworth knew this, and he was certain she would have disliked it intensely.

He had no intention, however, of allowing such unhappy

thoughts as these to overset his patient.

"You must rest easy and try to regain your strength so that you may go home as soon as possible," was his advice. "Doubtless, your husband will be here in less than a sennight, and then we shall see how you do."

That same afternoon a gentleman who gave his name as Edward Ainsworth arrived at his surgery. "I must confess that I was quite unprepared for you to arrive so soon as this," the doctor said. "Your sister had led me to believe that you were somewhere in the north and that you would not be able to return to London for several days after you received her message."

"That is true—at least, it was true as far she was cognizant of my whereabouts. I had made a journey to Yorkshire, following a rumor that my wife might have been the young lady who had been seen in that area. It was only the latest of many such rumors I have followed since she left our home. Believe me, rumors of that kind are so numerous that one would think half of England was populated with runaway young females."

Dr. Ward shook his head. "It is truly a sad situation. I trust the other young lady had also been identified?"

"She had not been when I came away." Mr. Ainsworth did not appear to have much concern for the unknown victim. "I felt there was nothing that I could do for her. Actually, despite the reports we had been given, she did not resemble my wife in the least, and was apparently a member of the servant class. Perhaps a bondmaid who was fleeing from her master. Someone of the sort, at any rate. Feeling depressed by having been led astray by another false rumor, I returned home today, to be greeted by the happy news that my sister had located my dear April, that she was here, under your care—but that you had refused to permit her to bring my wife home."

There was more than a hint of resentment in his tone, and the doctor was quick to explain. "Doubtless your sister reached a wrong conclusion about my reluctance."

He did not think anything of the kind; Miss Ainsworth had understood him quite well. However, it was not his custom to carry tales. The gentleman certainly must know of his sister's disposition.

"I thought I had explained my reasoning for the delay to her satisfaction, but I see that I must have been mistaken. It was merely that I thought I should discuss your wife's condition with you before I allowed her to leave my care."

As he spoke, the doctor was studying the other man, in order to ascertain to whom he would be entrusting his patient. He would have been concerned about anyone who had been in his care, but this young lady, he felt, needed especial attention because of her affliction.

He could see no resemblance to the lady who had called upon him earlier, but Dr. Ward knew that signified nothing, for members of a family often differed widely in appearance. He thought briefly of how little he resembled any members of his own family.

Edward Ainsworth was a slightly built gentleman of medium height—the doctor thought he would prove to be only an inch or two taller than his sister, who was of Amazonian proportions. He had brown hair and pale blue eyes, with none of the forceful gaze of his sister. It was doubtful that anyone would describe him as being a handsome man, but there were some ladies, Dr. Ward thought, who might find him appealing.

However, he received the impression that Mr. Ainsworth might be the sort of man who would permit himself to be guided by the lady who had come here earlier. She was probably several years older than her brother, and the doctor could see that she was the stronger-willed of the two. He could not decide how this would affect his patient. If the child was correct about the older woman's dislike of her . . .

Still, he knew that the girl would be happier among her own surroundings than if she remained with him. "I am certain your sister has told you that your wife is able to remember nothing whatever of her life until she woke here in my surgery. This is a result of the accident."

"Yes—I understand that she might not even recognize

me, that she did not know my sister. Of course, she has
not known Beatrix as long as she has known me, for I had
been a friend of her parents, but I still thought April should
have been able to recognize her. Since I feared that she
might not know me, either, and that you might have some
doubt that I was truly her husband, I have brought with me
the documents which will prove our relationship."

"That was not necessary," Dr. Ward told him, although
he held out his hand for the papers and began to peruse
them thoroughly.

The young gentleman appeared to feel there was further
need for him to explain the situation. "Perhaps, as you say, it
is not necessary, but, under the circumstances . . . I should
not like for you to receive the wrong impression about my
reason for being here. You will see by these papers that
my wife's parents had, for a number of years, been in
the habit of traveling extensively, taking her with them,
of course. They died in Paris, within a week of each
other."

"A tragedy indeed."

"It was, sir, and especially so for April, for she had
always been very close to them and felt their loss keenly.
As I said, I had been their nearest friend—one of their few
English friends remaining in France at this time. After their
deaths, I wished to bring April safely home, away from
the trouble there. My sister Beatrix had not accompanied
me on that journey, and you can understand that it would
have been most improper for a young lady to travel so
far with me alone; for her protection, we were married
in Paris."

"I see." The explanation did much to reassure Dr. Ward.
If the gentleman were as protective of her welfare as he
seemed, the doctor knew his patient would be in good hands
when he permitted her to leave.

"We were fortunate to be able to escape from Paris just
before the order went out to arrest all English. It was my
plan—and will be again, just as soon as she is able to
travel—to reunite April with her grandfather, the Earl of
Hannaford, who, I understand, has not seen her since she

was a small child. He had only the one son, and April is his only grandchild."

And quite probably his only heir, the doctor thought as he examined the documents. They were proofs of the death of Viscount and Lady Comber, and of the marriage of their daughter to Edward Ainsworth. Had his concern for the young lady's welfare been coupled with like concern for her possible fortune? It appeared probable to the doctor that it had been. Still, Ainsworth would certainly not be the first man who had married for money. There was nothing reprehensible about his having done such a thing.

"As you say, sir, these papers are quite in order. And your sister was certain of the identity of my patient. I should like you to verify that, of course, since you say your sister had not known her well."

"Of course. I am anxious to do so."

The doctor rose. "Before you see your wife, I must warn you that it may be some time before she recovers her memory."

"My sister has told me that you were unable to hold out any definite promise for the speed of my wife's recovery." He showed no sign of emotion at having been told this. Of course, if the marriage had been one of convenience, as he had implied, that could account for his demeanor. In any case, Dr. Ward thought it doubtful that Edward Ainsworth was the kind of man who would be much given to revealing his emotions.

"However," possibly Ainsworth sensed that the doctor expected him to display deeper feelings about his wife's condition, "I am hopeful that when she is reunited with those who love her, it will do much to ensure her rapid recovery from this sad condition."

"It is true, as I explained to Miss Ainsworth, that familiar surroundings can often do a great deal to spur the memory. However, it does not always prove to be the case. Your wife may recover completely by tomorrow—or it may take weeks for her to become herself. You understand that you must be patient with her."

"I can assure you, sir, that we shall see that she has the best of care."

"There is one other thing before you see her," Dr. Ward said. "She asks often about someone named Caroline. Can you tell me who that might be?"

"Possibly it may have been a childhood friend, some-one she might have met while traveling with her parents," Ainsworth answered. "Since I met with them only from time to time, I was not acquainted with all their other friends. I know of no one by that name, nor does Beatrix, I am certain."

Dr. Ward sighed. "That is a pity. The inability to recall anything about this Caroline frets her, and I had hoped you would be able to relieve her mind about her friend."

"I am sorry, but I cannot do so," Ainsworth continued. "There are times when April has slept poorly—a result of what she must have seen in France, I believe. It is at such times that she has most often mentioned the name and has appeared quite concerned about her welfare. I have prom-ised her to do what I can to locate this Caroline for her, but my efforts have been in vain. I am not certain that she still exists—or if she ever did."

"You say that her sleep has been disturbed?" The doctor made a note upon a paper he held.

"It is not surprising that it should have been, is it, when you remember that she must have seen many disturbing sights in France? Then there is the matter of her parents' death. That overset her more than I can tell you. It had not been suspected that they were so gravely ill that there was no chance for their recovery."

"You are right." Dr. Ward put the paper away, satisfied by the explanation. "Such a shock as that could cause a great disturbance of her thoughts, and may account in some part for her loss of memory. Her parents' deaths, just after her having seen the great destruction which has taken place in France . . . "

"Yes—I was not there as long as they, but much of what I saw was horrible beyond description," Ainsworth replied.

"As you say—there will doubtless be many things which

happened that she does not wish to remember so she has blanked out everything in her past. Although this sort of condition occurs quite often in children, it sometimes happens to adults, as well."

"You should know that in what we think must have been a moment of great stress—possibly while thinking about her parents—my wife started out while I was away from home; we believe it may have been in an effort to find the Caroline about whom she asks. Although what she thought she could accomplish when I have been able to find nothing, I do not know. She could not have been thinking clearly, only fretting about her unknown friend."

The doctor nodded, privately wondering if there might not have been some trouble between April and her sister-in-law while the gentleman was away. If that had been the case, and April had run off because of it, he doubted that Beatrix would have told her brother about it.

Ainsworth continued. "Beatrix did not know there was any reason for watching her closely, and she slipped away—we think with the aid of a servant. I assure you that once she is at home once more, I shall watch her carefully so that nothing of this sort occurs again."

"I am certain that you will do so, for you must not risk a repetition of her—shall we call it an escapade?" He could scarcely say, "and watch your sister as well, to see that they do not quarrel."

Again, Dr. Ward warned himself that it was certainly not his place to interfere in the private lives of others—except as it might affect his patient. And after all, he could be entirely wrong, since he could only judge by his patient's reluctance to be with her sister-in-law, a state which was not based on anything more than her imagination. "If it should happen again, she might not fare so well the next time."

"It does not seem that she has fared very well on this occasion, having been in so serious an accident," Ainsworth said soberly. "She might easily have been killed. You may be certain that I had no more idea than did my sister that she would attempt anything of this kind, or it would not have happened. Now, if I may see her—"

Once more, the doctor led a visitor to his patient's bedside, only to have her fix a puzzled look on the gentleman and ask, "Who are you?"

"April, my dear, I am Edward, your husband. The doctor has explained that you might not recognize me at first. When we have you at home again, however, I am certain you will remember. We want you to be completely well. And as quickly as possible. Now, doctor, I trust that you will have no objection if I bring a carriage to fetch my wife home today."

"I confess I shall be reluctant to lose her, for she has become dear to both my daughter and myself in the time she has been here. And, in view of what your sister told me, I thought to have several more days to observe her before allowing her to leave."

"Do you think that necessary?" For the first time, there was a touch of anxiety in his manner.

"No, it really is not." The doctor hastened to soothe the young man. "I must own that there is nothing more I can do for her, except to watch her for signs of her returning memory. You must promise, of course, to return her to my care without delay if she shows any indication of being disturbed by the move."

"Certainly, you may rest assured that I shall do so. After all, her well-being is my only concern. Now, if you will excuse me, I shall return with my sister and a carriage for my wife. We were living in the country at the time she left, but have thought it best to return to our London house for a time. It is not the season, so my wife should be able to live quietly until we feel she is able to go to visit her grandfather."

When he had left the room, the girl looked anxiously at the doctor and said, "Dr. Ward, are you quite certain that man is my husband? I cannot recall ever having seen him before."

The doctor restrained an impulse to smile at her remark and answered gravely, "My dear girl, you have no recollection of anyone in your life before your accident, so you would not recognize him."

"I suppose that is so," she said slowly.

"I am certain that he is your husband; he has the proofs of your parents' death and of your marriage. There would be no reason for him to pretend that he had an interest in you if it were not so. And I assure you, my dear child, that I should not release you to his care unless I was certain it was for your best interest."

"Very well, if you say so, I shall have to go with him. And with Beatrix, too, I suppose." These last words were said without enthusiasm, as if she did not gladly anticipate the meeting.

Chapter Three

It was a pity that she had apparently taken an instant dislike to her sister-in-law. Instant, because she could have no recollection of having seen her before. The doctor had the feeling that Miss Ainsworth was the sort of female who would rule the household—but his patient would have no way of knowing about that, either. He took comfort in knowing the few sentences Miss Ainsworth had exchanged with the girl showed nothing but deepest consideration for her welfare.

Was it possible that there might be at least a glimmer of returning memory? He shook his head; the girl's obvious reluctance to go with the older lady meant nothing of the kind, he was certain.

He had thought that Miss Ainsworth might have been somewhat impatient with her sister-in-law because of her escapade—for had she not implied that the girl had run away from home? It could be that the child—for he was unable to think of her as being much more than that—had sensed this impatience. Like a child, she doubtless expected and dreaded a scolding for what she had done, even though she could not remember her reason for doing so.

"Yes," he said, "he is bringing his sister to help you. Now, we must prepare you for leaving here."

Barely half an hour later, Edward and Beatrix Ainsworth returned for April. "Is it necessary for my wife to remain in bed?" Mr. Ainsworth asked. "Or would it be a good thing if she were able to move about?"

"No—that is, she need not remain in bed. Physically, there is nothing whatever the matter with her now, except for the bruise from the fall that has caused her loss of memory. There will still be some tenderness at that spot, and you should guard that area, but the few other bruises she suffered have almost completely gone and should give her no pain."

"That is good. I can see that you have given her the best of care, doctor."

"Only the same care any of my patients receive, Mr. Ainsworth. In answer to your question, moving about should do her good rather than harm. She has been permitted to walk around here from time to time, as I approve of light exercise for my patients. You will notice that I said *light;* I should not suggest that, for some time, you permit her to take any sort of strenuous exercise. That might cause a setback in her condition."

Both brother and sister assured him at once that they wanted to do only what was best for April. Watching them assist the girl into the carriage and tuck the rugs carefully about her, the doctor smiled and sighed. Sighed, because he would have liked to be permitted to keep her where he could observe her progress, for such cases did not often fall to his lot. Too, as he had said, he had grown fond of her.

There was no doubt, however, that her chances of speedily recovering her memory would be much better if she were at home, among familiar objects and with people who cared for her, and the thought of her recovery brought a smile. He wondered if he would see her again, but doubted the Ainsworths would wish to return to this neighborhood when it was not necessary.

"The doctor said you might move about, as long as you

take care not to attempt too much," Edward said to her when they arrived home. At least, both of them had told her it was home, but everything about the house was quite as strange to April as were the two people who had brought her here. Still, they insisted this was her home, so she hoped she would soon begin to recognize it.

She stifled a wish that she could once more be in the doctor's care, back with the only two people she trusted. There she had felt safe—but she told herself it was because all this was strange to her at present. She would doubtless like her home better, as soon as she remembered it.

"However," Edward continued, "I think it might be the the best thing for you to rest now. This is the first time you have been so long out of your bed, and the carriage ride must have tired you."

"Yes," Beatrix agreed. "Come along, dear. You do look quite pale. I shall tuck you up at once and see that you have a light dinner in bed."

As she led the girl away, April looked back to where Edward was standing, watching them. She was a bit anxious about going upstairs alone with Beatrix, although she did not know why it should be so.

"I shall come up later to bid you good night," he said. She wondered if he sensed her uneasiness about being alone with Beatrix.

He added reassuringly, "But you need not worry about one thing, at least, for the present. Our marriage—although you may not recall anything about it—took place merely for your protection while we left France. I shall not expect anything of you. All I wish now is to return you safely to the care of your grandfather."

"Yes, I—understand." Truly, April was not certain that she did understand. And she did not know whether to be happy that Edward had no intention of being a true husband to her, since she did not know what the words implied. *Perhaps I should have asked the doctor what it means to have a husband*, she thought. *He would understand that all this would be strange to me.* She sensed that Beatrix was pleased that Edward did not intend to act as her husband.

She was far too tired, however, to concern herself just now about such matters. Perhaps, as they said, she was still weak due to her accident and the carriage ride had wearied her. Beatrix had brought her a robe and nightgown of her own, which were much too long, but since she would be wearing them only in bed the additional length scarcely mattered. She only nibbled at a light dinner, and was fast asleep before Beatrix and the maid had left the room.

April awoke with soft sunlight filtering through the rose-colored curtains and falling across her face. She had slept soundly from the late afternoon until this moment, with none of her occasional shadowy dreams to disturb her.

For some moments longer she lay with her eyes closed, content merely to enjoy the warmth, which felt so good after the days she had spent in the doctor's tiny room. Everything had been so white and neat, with no fripperies of any sort. The bed there had been comfortable enough, but it had not been nearly as soft or spacious as this one. "This bed," she murmured, and laughed at the thought, "would have crowded that small room until no one could have entered it."

Opening her eyes, she looked about her present room. As far as she could tell, it was decorated in a manner which spoke of wealth and good taste, from the rich curtains—which she had sleepily insisted should not be closed—framing her feather-soft bed, to the matching window draperies to the carved and gilded furniture scattered about. It was such a beautiful room, but for the moment she forgot why she was here and not at the surgery.

Then she remembered what had happened to her in the past several days. But the pain of being nameless, more painful than her physical injuries, was a thing of the past. She now knew who she was, and where; of course, this was only what she had been told, but she knew it must be true. Even Beatrix, who seemed to have no reason for liking her, would not lie to her about such a thing.

For some reason she could not understand, she felt that Beatrix would have preferred *not* to have her here, but told herself she must be wrong. After all Beatrix had helped to bring her home and had tucked her into bed, wishing her a good night. April quickly dismissed her uneasy feeling about her sister-in-law, choosing instead to feel happy about knowing who she was.

"I am April Ainsworth," she said aloud, liking the sound of the words, liking the assurance she received from knowing who she was. Her husband—husband in name only, he had assured her, although she still wondered about the meaning of the term—and his sister Beatrix had come to the doctor's surgery yesterday and had brought her home. She had been told that they had been living in the country when she ran away, but that they had spent some time in London when they first arrived from France.

This was her husband's house—which meant, of course, that it was her own. She was told she had lived here for a time, and yet nothing had appeared the least bit familiar to her. But then, she told herself, she could remember nothing at all about her life until she had roused to see Helen Ward's pleasant face bending over her.

"Perhaps, now that I am home, everything will come back to me," she said, not bothering to stifle a yawn. Not that she was still sleepy, merely delightfully lazy.

It was comforting to know that, even if she could recognize nothing, she was once more with people who cared for her. And, as far as she had been able to judge from the brief glimpse of her surroundings, they were people who lived in some luxury. As she must have—even if she could not recall anything about it.

"I hope I will begin to remember—and soon. It is so disconcerting to be as I now am, as if I had never existed until this time."

Her musings were interrupted by the sound of soft scratching at the door and, almost automatically, she said, "Come in."

The same black-haired, pink-cheeked young maid who had served her dinner last evening entered the room, carrying her breakfast tray. "I hope that you have rested well, Mrs. Ainsworth," the girl said cheerfully. "And I hope 'twas not wrong of me to come so soon. Perhaps I ought to have waited until you rang for breakfast."

"No—no, it is quite all right. I never thought of ringing. But I am certain it is time I awoke—and I own that I *am* hungry."

"That is good. And if I am not being too bold, Madam, I'd like to say that all of us are so happy that you are at home once more."

"Thank you—Lucy, is it not?" At least she had a memory for things since her accident. There could be nothing seriously wrong with her mind if she could do that. She hoped it might be a sign that her memory was beginning to return.

"Yes, Madam, Lucy—Lucy Martin. Burrows tells me that I must become accustomed to having everyone call me Martin, but it is so difficult for me to do that, for no one has ever done that. You see, this is the very first position I have had. My Mam kept me at home until my younger sister was big enough to help out with the babes. You see, there were four brothers between us, so she is still little more than a babe herself."

Fortunately, she had set the breakfast tray on the table beside the bed, or she would certainly have dropped it as she put both hands over her mouth. She had suddenly realized that she was chattering with the mistress, something she had been strictly ordered that she must never do. Servants, she had been told, were not to speak unless their betters wished them to do so.

April recalled that, last evening, the girl had seemed to be nervous when serving her and helping her to undress. However, if she was somewhat new to service, that was no more than one might expect. Especially when she must do her work under Beatrix' critical eye.

Just now, however, there was something she felt she ought to know. "Burrows? Who is that?"

"Why, Burrows is the butler, Madam." What a question that was. After all, Burrows must have been with the family *forever*. Asking who he was was almost like asking the name of the Thames River.

Seeing the puzzled expression her question had brought to the girl's face, April felt she was obliged to offer her an explanation. "You see, Lucy—when we are alone, I think I should like to call you Lucy, if you will not mind my doing so; Martin seems to be much too formal between the two of us, and you say you are not accustomed to it—I have been in a serious accident and I can remember nothing about myself or my life."

"Oh, Madam, how awful that must be for you!" The girl's face puckered in sympathy.

April nodded, happy to discover that the movement no longer caused her pain. At least, that part of her condition appeared to have improved a great deal in the few hours that she had been home. "Yes, it is. Quite a dreadful feeling. They—the doctor, as well as my husband and Beatrix—tell me that my memory will return soon, and I hope they may be right. It seems unbelievable, but I could not recognize Mr. Ainsworth or his sister when they came to take me home. I cannot even remember you."

It did not seem odd to her that she ought to be able to remember her maid when she could not remember her husband or her sister-in-law. She had a feeling—ungrateful though it might be toward one who had shown nothing but kindness to her—that she would be pleased not to have to remember Beatrix.

"Oh, there is no way that you could remember me," Lucy said quickly. "I only came to work here three days ago, and of course, you were not here then."

She had been dreading her first meeting with her new mistress. She had no previous experience with the Quality, but Miss Ainsworth, who had employed her, appeared to be such a lofty person and nearly impossible to please, and she had feared the mistress would be much like her.

Instead, the young lady was so much more soft-spoken, even wanting to call her "Lucy." She felt that she had found a friend in this strange place. It would be a pleasure to serve so nice a lady, and she hoped she would do nothing to earn dismissal, as the girl before her had done.

With only the briefest of raps, Beatrix came into the room. She frowned when she saw the maid was still present, but only said, "You may return in half an hour, Martin, and help your mistress to dress."

Lucy curtsied and withdrew. Outside the closed door, she grimaced and muttered, "Old cat. I would wager she will give that poor girl a hard time. 'Tis no wonder to me that she ran away, if that is what she has had to live with every day."

In the room she had left, Beatrix was saying, "I simply cannot understand why you must treat the servants in such a familiar manner, April. Doubtless, it is something you were accustomed to doing when you traveled with your parents. I have heard that some foreign countries have odd customs."

"I do not—"

"But you are in England now, not in Paris, and matters are handled quite differently here. You must not forget—again—that you are Mrs. Edward Ainsworth, as well as being the granddaughter of the Earl of Hannaford, and you must remember to conduct yourself accordingly. At all times."

"Yes, Beatrix, I shall try to remember." It was a waste of words to attempt to argue with her. Too, it might be that she was right.

"Yes, it is important for you to do so. There will be times, after you have met your grandfather, that you will be introduced to people of rank. You may be presented at court. I should imagine that an old man such as your grandfather would be more interested in receiving the approval of Their Majesties than in the opinions of the raffish group around the Prince Regent."

April nodded. None of this meant anything to her, but Beatrix seemed to think it important.

"Such casual behavior as you have been displaying toward members of the lower orders is completely unacceptable. It gives them ideas above their station."

For a moment, she was tempted to retort that it was she, and not Beatrix, who was mistress in her husband's home, and that she would treat the servants as she liked. She could not be certain, however, that Beatrix was not within her rights to dictate how she should behave. It was so discouraging not to know what she ought to do.

Why does she dislike me as she does? What could I have done to make her feel this way? April thought to herself. She had thought earlier that she was being ungrateful to think that Beatrix did not like her when she had shown her only kindness. Now she could tell that the kindness had been merely on the surface, possibly laid on to impress the doctor. Beatrix truly *did* resent her being here.

"Yes, Beatrix," she said humbly. "I shall attempt to remember that much. I was only questioning her because I thought I ought to know my own maid. She tells me she is new here."

"Certainly, she is a new girl. Your former maid had to be dismissed without a character. We could scarcely allow her to remain in our service, after she had helped you to run away. You see, April, that in addition to the pain it has given us, your naughtiness has cost that girl a much-needed position."

"Oh, it is so unfair to hold her to blame for what happened. I do not remember anything about the time before I—I left, of course, but certainly I must have ordered her to do as she did, so she would have had to obey me. Can you not give her another chance?" Could she insist on it? She did not know, but doubted Beatrix would listen to her even if she did.

"We can hardly bring her back into our household." The tone in which her sister-in-law spoke proved to April that she had been right; Beatrix would be the one to decide what was done about the servants. "To do so would be to admit to the rest of the staff that we did not see anything wrong in her behavior, and we cannot permit them to think that—it makes them lax. I have been trying to tell you that they are always far too prompt take advantage of such treatment."

April could not help wondering if servants were truly as unworthy as Beatrix said. Lucy had appeared to be quite concerned about her welfare—surely that was not a sign of laxness. And her former maid—what *was* her name?— must have been willing to assist her in whatever it was that she had been planning when she left home. She must have been more a friend than a servant.

As if reading her mind, Beatrix continued, "The old girl would not have dared do anything of the kind had you been as strict with her as you ought. She deserved to be sent packing for acting as she did, and one hopes it will prove a lesson to her, not to behave in such a manner in the future. I shall, however, attempt to find her another position, if that will make you happy."

"That would be kind of you, Beatrix," the younger woman said humbly, thankful for even this concession on the other's part. "And it would ease my conscience if you were to do so."

"Yes." Beatrix' tone was sharp. "You must have quite enough on your conscience already, for having been the cause of so much anguish to Edward, and to me as well, when we did not know where you might have gone. I cannot see what made you do so thoughtless a thing as that. I suppose you were off somewhere in search of that mysterious Caroline you speak about so often. I truly doubt if such a person exists outside of your imagination."

"Oh, I feel that she must—"

"You do not know whether she does or not. But that is of no importance at this time. When you are dressed, we must take you shopping. Edward has made enquiries since we knew where you were injured, but not one piece of your luggage has been recovered."

"That is too bad." April felt that she was expected to say something in answer to the censure in Beatrix' voice. "Although, I suppose in this time—"

"Yes, it is a pity to lose so many of your things. A number of them were quite good, of course—although you had left behind one or two small pieces of jewelry. Fortunately, we had not had time to purchase much in that line, so little was lost. I suppose someone saw an excellent opportunity to deck his sweetheart out in your finery. Since you took everything else you possessed, it seemed to us that you were planning *not* to return. I simply cannot understand why you should wish to cause so much grief for Edward."

"I cannot remember—"

"And for me, although I doubt that you feel you have any

reason to consider my feelings. The gown you were wearing at the time of your accident was one you had borrowed from your maid—completely unsuited, of course, for a lady of your position. So now you must be entirely outfitted—again."

"Yes, Beatrix." It was easier to agree with whatever Beatrix said than to risk another scolding. Especially when she could not be certain whether she had truly done something wrong, or whether it was only Beatrix' customary disapproval of her. Had she truly been so inconsiderate of her sister-in-law's feelings before, or was that merely another excuse for Beatrix to berate her?

Under Beatrix' watchful eye, a subdued Lucy aided April to dress. Her gown had been cleaned, pressed and mended, first by Helen Ward, then—as if the work had not been good enough for an Ainsworth—again by the servants here. However, it was a blue kerseymere, so badly faded by many washings that it was almost gray, and clearly had not been of the best quality even when it had been new. April supposed her sister-in-law must be right in saying she had borrowed it from her maid, and she could imagine how the servants must have sneered over it as they cleaned it for her.

She knew how Lucy must be feeling about the constant scoldings she was receiving; nothing she did seemed to please Beatrix. April's feelings were much the same as the maid's—Beatrix *was* quite overbearing in many ways. Doubtless, she had made a home for her brother for a number of years, and must naturally resent now having to take second place to someone else.

Or would she ever take second place? April wondered. *She probably preferred that spot for me—if she had to have me here at all.* Even though April knew Edward had married her only out of friendship for her parents, so that he might bring her safely out of France, his bride surely would have been unwanted by Beatrix.

Whatever her sister-in-law's feeling about her might be, however, she was clearly determined that April should be gowned as befitting her present position. *Could I truly have managed to carry away so many clothes when I left?* April wondered, as the pair spent hour after hour in various shops along Bond Street, choosing everything from gowns and bonnets to matching reticules, shoes, and parasols. Dozens of pairs of colored gloves and an equal supply of silk stockings of various tints were added to their purchases before Beatrix decided that April now had what she might need for the near future.

April wished she could have spoken to some of the fashionable ladies that they saw in the shops—but even if Beatrix had given her the time to do so, she did not think she would have known what to say and would have appeared quite stupid. It was just as well that she had not had the chance to speak.

"We can purchase more things for you later, when we have the time," Beatrix told her as they started home, "but, after all, we shall soon be presenting you to your grandfather for the first time in many years, and it will not do to have him think that your husband has stinted you in any way. It is a pity that we could not persuade Madame Bertin to outfit you; her style is always recognizable."

April nodded. She realized that she knew nothing at all about the fashions of the day, but even she could see how Madame's gowns stood out above the others. She wondered if her grandfather would have known the difference—but perhaps there would be others at his home who would.

"But we could not afford so long a wait at this time. She has so many clients that one must make appointments with her weeks ahead. And since she does not now know who you are, it would be impossible to expect her to put clients of long standing aside for you. Later, when you have taken your proper place in the ton, she will doubtless attempt to curry your favor. Still, I think we managed to do quite well at some of the other shops."

"Yes, Beatrix." *How many times today have I said those two dreadful words?* April asked herself. Would she continue to allow herself to be dominated by Beatrix, even after she had reached her grandfather's home and had been reintroduced to him? Or would the old gentleman—whom she could not remember, and who had evidently not seen her since she was a child—stand between her and Beatrix? Somehow, she had the feeling that her husband would not.

Among the gowns which needed no alterations was one of a soft rose-colored crepe lisse with bandings of a deeper hue about the skirt. It was April's favorite of all her new things, but Beatrix waved it aside and suggested—in a tone which April considered tantamount to a command—that she wear instead a gown of pale lilac jaconet, bound at the waist with ribbons of a darker shade and bows of the same ribbon from waistline to hem.

Chapter Four

"This gown will be perfect for someone with your fair hair and pale skin," Beatrix declared, spreading it out upon the bed.

April thought that she was far too pallid—whether this was natural or the result of her illness, she did not know—and that the rose shade would have added a bit more color to her face than the lilac. As usual, however, she found that she was unable to argue with the older woman. Beatrix would never have listened to her suggestion that she would like to wear the other gown, she was certain. If Beatrix decreed lilac, that was what she must wear.

Dutifully, she allowed Lucy to slip the lilac gown over her head and twitch it into place, then fasten the many buttons down the back. It *was* a pretty gown, she owned to herself, and it fitted her quite as well as the other but, although she could have given no reason for her choice, she would have preferred to wear the rose-colored one.

Without commenting upon April's appearance in the new gown—which unfortunately gave her a becoming air of fragility that the older woman did not like—Beatrix was continuing her list of instructions. "I think we might consider dispensing with that ugly bandage around your head now that you are at home, since the doctor has said the bruise itself is no longer a serious one and is only a bit tender. It should do no harm to leave it uncovered, for it is not like a sore finger that you would forever be striking against something. Now, we shall see if Martin is as good as she claims to be at arranging a lady's hair."

Clearly nervous under Miss Ainsworth's watchful gaze, Lucy nonetheless whisked away the bandage and, finding April's soft hair so easy to manage, contrived a simple arrangement that covered the bruise. April was pleased with the result of her efforts and told her so.

"I suppose that it must do for the present," Beatrix owned, as if reluctant to agree with anything April liked, "even if it is not a fashionable style. At least, it serves to hide that ugly mark upon your head, which is the best thing one can say about it. Once that has faded a bit, we shall have to see what we can do about a more satisfactory arrangement."

"But I like—"

"It might be well to send for a competent hairdresser to come and demonstrate what should be done. I trust that even Martin should be able to follow simple directions in the future. Now, Martin, do make haste with the rest of Mrs. Ainsworth's preparations. Edward will be dining at home this evening, April, and, as this is your first evening at home, it would not be right to keep him waiting."

"Of course, Beatrix, I should not wish to do so, but I am certain I can manage the rest myself without Lu—Martin's help."

Beatrix made no reply, but her look was so censorious that Lucy bobbed a quick curtsy and said, "Oh no, miss— I mean Madam. That will not be necessary. I can do everything for you within a few moments."

"Then see that you do so with no more dawdling." The sharp remark showed that not even the maid's hasty agreement had been enough to overcome Beatrix' obvious distaste at April's having dared to disagree with her order. "Now, I must go and dress at once, for I have already wasted far too much time." *Wasted while I vainly attempted to make you presentable,* was the implication—well understood by both mistress and maid.

"Fortunately, Evans is both capable and speedy, so I ought not to be late. Dinner will be served in half an hour, April, so it would be the best thing for you to go down in twenty minutes, so that Edward will have an opportunity to see how much we have accomplished today."

"Yes, Beatrix." As soon as the door had closed behind the older lady, April and Lucy looked at one another and exchanged rather guilty grins. They were about the same age, Lucy perhaps a year older than April, but both young enough to feel a sense of rebellion at the continuous orders Beatrix threw at them.

Lucy had been told frequently since she came here that as a servant, especially a lady's maid in such a great house as this, she had no right to resent whatever her employer might say to her. Ladies felt that they had been given the privilege of being capricious and the maidservants must accept the fact. Still, she had quickly come to feel that young Mrs. Ainsworth was nothing like that. The young lady seemed to regard her almost as friend, unlike her sister-in-law, whom she thought a terror.

How can the young lady and her husband have a chance to be happy as long as they have that dragon striding about the place, finding fault with what is being done all the time? she asked herself, as she knelt beside her mistress to help her into a pair of new kid slippers and to see that the clocks in her lilac silk stockings were quite straight.

How the old catamount would rail at the pair of them if something of that kind was overlooked! She might even decide that Mrs. Ainsworth needed a more experienced abigail. Lucy felt that any amount of scolding from the older woman would mean nothing as long as she could remain with the younger one.

April smoothed her dress as Lucy finished her ministrations. As much as she disliked being forced to listen to her sister-in-law's constant criticism, April could not fail to wish that she might have waited for Beatrix to complete her dressing, so that they might have gone downstairs together. Since her only memory of her husband was their meeting at the doctor's surgery and their few words upon returning home, she felt that she would be greeting a stranger. However, Beatrix had told—ordered—her to go down, so she had no choice but to do so.

She walked slowly down the steps, hesitating before she entered the drawing room, unwilling to admit, even to herself, that she lacked the courage to approach her husband. Edward looked very grand in his dark green colored dinner coat this evening, with his hair brushed to a smooth cap, and with his snowy cravat tied in an intricate knot.

April wondered how he could have chosen her from all the elegant ladies he must have known. She had been told, by Beatrix as well as by Edward, that he had married her only for her own protection on the way from Paris, but it seemed to her that he surely he could have managed her return in some other way than by marrying her, had he wished to do so.

Despite Beatrix' implication that he certainly could have had no other reason for showing her such kindness, April thought that perhaps it had not been done *entirely* for her protection. She hoped she would find that he had some slight feeling for her.

The admiration she saw in Edward's eyes as he came to meet her and draw her into the room soon reassured her, and the hand in which he had imprisoned hers was comforting. "In so short a time, I had almost forgot how lovely you are," he said in a tone so warm that April felt herself flushing with pleasure. She had been right to hope; he did not find her unpleasing.

"Beatrix chose this gown for me," she said to cover her confusion.

"Yes, Bea has excellent taste."

Although she owned to herself that he was doubtless right about the matter, his enthusiastic praise of his sister rankled somewhat. Perhaps, she said to herself, she was being unreasonable, but it seemed to her that as his wife it should be *she* who was given his praise for the manner in which she dressed. Perhaps for other things, as well. She was not quite certain, however, what would be the best way for her to win it.

"I should have preferred to wear a rose-colored gown today, rather than this one," she told him, hoping she would not sound as if she was complaining about her sister-in-law, even if that was what she was doing, "but this was her choice."

"Rose—" He studied her, head tipped a bit one side, then gave her the praise she had wished. "Yes, you would look equally well in rose. In fact, it would doubtless have been more attractive on you than this. The color is one of my favorites."

So that is why Beatrix did not wish for me to wear the rose-colored one, April thought, remembering that the older woman had hesitated for some moments before allowing her to add that particular gown to her wardrobe, despite— or could it have been because of—the way the dressmaker and her assistants had praised April's appearance in it. She gathered that she would not have been allowed to take it if there had been more gowns available upon such short notice.

Her feeling about her sister-in-law had been correct, too. Beatrix *was* jealous of any attention Edward might pay to his wife. The thought made April smile up at him with renewed confidence.

"Yes," he repeated, in a tone so ardent that April felt herself flushing with pleasure, "you are lovely tonight, my dear—very lovely."

He still had her hand in his, a fact which Beatrix could not fail to notice as she descended the stairs and entered the room. "I see you approve of my choice for a gown for the child, Edward." Her tone was crisp, hiding the anger she felt at this sign that it was the girl, not the gown, of whom Edward approved.

Beatrix knew quite well his true reason for having married April—or at least, the reason he had given her—but she had wondered at the time if there might have been another reason for the marriage, as well. His evident admiration for the girl at the present time had a most disquieting effect upon her.

If only I could have walked away and left her with the doctor, never telling Edward she was there, she said to herself as she continued aloud, "I may as well tell you that it was not the one she would have worn this evening, if I had let her choose. But I convinced her that this is what you would prefer."

"No, she has told me she wanted to wear rose," he said, quickly dropping the hand he had been holding, going to meet his sister and to take her hand instead. "But you are right, Bea, as you always are. I am certain this becomes her much better than the other could do."

That is not what you told me a moment or two ago, April said to herself. Could it be that Edward was actually *afraid* of his sister, afraid to offend her feelings by expressing his own? April would not have thought it of him. True, Beatrix was able to frighten her at times—but Edward was a man. Surely he should not permit his sister to dictate what he should do.

Or perhaps his present agreement with Beatrix' opinion was merely his effort to keep the peace between the members of his family. He had married April in order to bring her safely home; at least, that was what he and Beatrix had told her. He may have thought it best to do anything possible to mollify the older woman, who obviously did not approve of his making such a match, however she might be forced to pretend that she did so.

Nonetheless, there was nothing Beatrix could do once the marriage had been solemnized, aside from criticizing whatever her sister-in-law might wish to do or say. April smiled again.

"Good evening, Beatrix," she said demurely. "Your gown is beautiful. I wish I could wear such a gown as that, but I know it would never do for me."

"No, you are entirely the wrong type of person for a gown of this sort." There was pride, perhaps a hint of smugness in Beatrix' tone, the praise making her forget for a moment the strong resentment she felt toward the other. Her dinner gown was the exact shade of her deep auburn hair; only someone of complete self-assurance would have dared to wear such a color.

April wondered, however, if the decolletage was not a rather extreme choice for a simple dinner at home with no one except her family. The diamond necklace she wore— also out of place on so simple an occasion—did nothing to mask her throat and the upper curves of her bosom. Yet on Beatrix' form—"queenly" was the only description which came to the girl's mind—the effect of the brilliant gown fitting her snugly from her shoulders almost to her knees, and the expanse of creamy skin which was revealed by the unusually low neckline were a striking combination. While she suspected that Beatrix had planned matters in this way, April knew that, beside the other, she faded into insignificance.

It was quite clear that Edward agreed with her. "You are magnificent tonight, Bea. But then you always are. It is good that April has the benefit of your advice. With your guidance, we shall be able to present her to the Earl of Hannaford in the style his granddaughter should display."

Beatrix threw her sister-in-law a mocking glance, as if to say, "You can see which of us counts for the most in Edward's life," but April doubted she would *say* anything of the kind—at least, in her brother's presence. Whatever Beatrix might have intended, she was prevented from making any further remarks by the arrival of Burrows to announce dinner.

Edward offered his arm to his sister, rather than to his wife. As April trailed after the two of them into the dining room, she wondered if this was the way it was always to be. Was he merely being polite to Beatrix because she was the elder, or, as it was increasingly easy for April to believe, would she always be forced to stand in the shadow of Beatrix, never to be accorded her proper place as mistress of the house?

"Of course," she murmured so that they could not hear, "Beatrix *did* tell me that Edward had married me after my parents died, only because it was not the proper thing for an unmarried girl to travel alone with a gentleman. And he told me the same. I thought he might have at least a bit of fondness for me to have done such a thing to help me, but now I can see I must have been mistaken. His only plan now seems to be to deliver me as quickly as he can to my grandfather. I suppose he will be happy when he can hand me over and forget that he has ever seen me." Beatrix would be happy on that occasion, she was certain.

"And now that you two have completed your shopping, how soon may we be able to make our bid to Hannaford?" Edward's question, which proved that April was correct in thinking he was anxious to hand her over to the earl, had been addressed to his sister, of course. April supposed that she was not to be consulted about whether or not she preferred to go to her grandfather. They had decided she would go, so the matter had been settled. Her sister-in-law and her husband could not wait to rid themselves of her, she told herself.

"We cannot do so for at least another sennight, I fear. Everything *should* be finished by that time." Beatrix' tone threatened dire consequences to the couturiere if they were not. "We were only able to find a few gowns that April could wear at once or with only minor alterations."

"I can understand that such things would take some time, but—"

"A great deal of time, I can tell you. Seamstresses are always so slow, it would seem."

April thought they would be working very fast, when one considered all they must do, but supposed she must be wrong again, since Beatrix disagreed.

"Bertin would not take us at all, of course," Beatrix was continuing her complaint, "on such short notice as we were able to give her. Especially when she saw April in that servant's gown and realized that she would be expected to make her look like a lady. Perhaps she thought that was even beyond *her* power."

Edward looked up from his plate. "Oh, it was not that bad—"

Beatrix would not permit interruptions, even from him. "Most of the gowns we were able to find will require a great deal of work to make them fit April. The greater number of them, of course, must be made from whole cloth. In a way, it is a pity that she is so small."

Edward nodded acceptance of this statement, and April lowered her eyes so that the others could not see the gleam of satisfaction she knew she was unable to hide. It was only, the couturiere had told them this afternoon, because Mrs. Ainsworth was so petite that they had been able to fit her at once.

"If the gowns were for yourself," she had told Beatrix, "I only could fit you today and have you return in a sennight or so for the first of your gowns. And a complete order of this size—for you—would have taken several weeks to make up."

"*My* wardrobe is complete, woman," Beatrix had told her stiffly.

"That is good," the couturiere was completely unmoved by the criticism in Beatrix' voice; she was well accustomed to dealing with members of the Quality, and knew herself to be essential to their success, "for the only gowns I have even partially finished which would fit you have been made for dowagers, but I have three gowns already made up which Mrs. Ainsworth can wear with the addition of only a stitch or two, and another which will require shortening. The others you wish will be ready next week."

Naturally, Beatrix was not about to tell her brother any of this, especially the part where the fitter said her size approximated that of the dowagers. Instead, she only allowed him to think that it was because of April's small stature, rather than because of the size of their order, that they must wait.

Edward would accept Beatrix' word about this, as he did about all else. After all, April told herself, it was not to be expected that a gentleman would know what went on in a dressmaker's establishment. Not unless he was the type who was well accustomed to purchasing a lady's clothes— which, it was clear to her, Edward was not.

"Well, if we must wait, we must," he said with a shrug. "Certainly, we cannot take April to her grandfather looking like a ragamuffin—which, I must confess, my child, you did when we found you."

"I suppose that my luggage must have been lost at the time of the accident." April knew that both of them must hold her to blame for being the cause of so great a loss, since she had—as far as she had been told—run off alone.

Beatrix scowled, either at the thought of so great a loss, or of the considerable expense and the effort on her part it had taken to replace the clothing. Edward, however, merely shrugged, commenting, "Well, that is something which cannot be helped now. And another sennight's delay does not matter too greatly since we have found you again. It will allow you more time to regain your strength. I shall send word to Lord Hannaford, so that he may expect to receive us then. I know how eager he must be to be reunited with his only granddaughter."

"Yes, and April will be quite as happy to see him again, will you not, April?" Ignoring the fact that the girl could not remember ever having met the old gentleman, and so could not know whether any such meeting would be enjoyable or quite the opposite, Beatrix patted her hand as they rose from the table.

"Yes, Beatrix." When she was acknowledged as the earl's granddaughter—if he should decide to accept her—would she be able to stop saying those two words? Words which had, in these few days, become so hateful to her. It seemed to her that they were becoming a sign of her servitude to Beatrix.

The only thought she could hug to herself was that while she could never have worn the exotic gown Beatrix had donned for dinner, neither could the auburn-haired woman have dared to appear in the shade of rose-pink April liked so well, and which Edward owned was a favorite of his. With hair of Beatrix' color, the gown would have looked horrible.

At the end of the waiting period, when all of April's new gowns and fripperies had been delivered and pronounced suitable—her sister-in-law would give them no more praise than that, although April thought them delightful—they were carefully folded and packed by Lucy, according to almost interminable instructions from Beatrix. The entourage was then away on the journey to Silver Acres, as the earl's ancestor had named his estate in honor of the great hoard of silver he had gained while raiding Spanish vessels in the service of Queen Elizabeth.

It had several times been rumored—although certainly never in Her Majesty's hearing, for such a tale would have been fatal to the privateer—that he had been able to put aside for himself nearly as much as he delivered to the throne. How else could he have afforded so grand an estate?

Edward, Beatrix, and April occupied the first carriage, followed by one which lacked the fresh paint and silver trim of the first. It carried Lucy, along with Purdom, Edward's valet, and Evans, Beatrix' dresser. The woman felt herself to be quite as superior as did her mistress, and was equally accustomed to treating Lucy as if she was of no more importance than a kitchen maid.

After them came a third coach, heavily laden with their luggage. Edward and Beatrix had discussed—overlooking April's opinions as they were in the habit of doing—whether or not it would be wise for them to employ outriders for the journey, but decided at last that this might be considered too ostentatious of them to make such a display at this time.

"After April has been acknowledged as Hannaford's heiress, it will be a different matter, of course," Beatrix had declared. "Her position then—and yours, of course, as her husband—may make such an entourage necessary." As always, it was her opinion which settled the question.

"If Hannaford could manage to get a title for her, we could also have a crest upon the doors," Edward told her. "If she pleases him—and I have no doubt she will—he may do so. Or do you think it would be appropriate for her to use his crest?"

"I fear I have no idea about that," Beatrix said, (*she actually admits there is something she does not know,* April

thought) "but we can certainly look into the matter. It would
be nice indeed to have a carriage with a crest."

*Doubtless, they would have preferred to have me ride
with the servants, had it not been that such an action would
have caused talk,* April thought to herself. *Their talk of my
having a crest for my carriage is for their benefit, not for
mine.* She felt much the same as when Beatrix had talked
about the important people April might meet. It would be
to their advantage if the earl agreed to have her presented
at court. She wondered what would be involved in such a
presentation, but thought it just as well not to ask. Neither
of them truly cared enough to tell her.

She might as well have been riding with the servants for
all the attention she received from either of the pair. It
seemed to her that she was only the means for Edward and
Beatrix to realize their ambitions of wealth—much greater
wealth than they now possessed.

However, aside from their discussion about the crest,
April scarcely listened to what the others were saying.
Her mind was on the end of their journey. She could
not remember her mother or father—perhaps her memory
would return soon, and she could again see them as they
had been in life. As for the old gentleman they were going
to see, he could never have been much more than a name
to her, if her parents had traveled for so many years.

For several days, they passed through some of the loveliest
scenery in England, great expanses of fertile fields bounded
by flowering hedgerows, with forests here and there. However, April was able to give but little attention to the beauty
of the countryside through which they were traveling.

The hills and forests would not have been familiar to her
in any case, but she was far more concerned with the end
of their journey than with scenery. As the carriages passed
through the enormous stone gateposts that marked the edge
of the long drive and wound their way between ancient oak
trees toward the earl's mansion, she experienced a sudden
feeling of terror.

Edward only wished to deliver her to her grandfather. But
what if the old gentleman did not wish to see her after all?

He might have quarreled with his son and disowned him. That would account for the couple's long journeys about the Continent.

If Edward's only wish was to rid himself of her as quickly as he could do so—as she was certain *Beatrix* wished— and if her grandfather would not receive her, what was she to do?

Chapter Five

The dark shadows cast over the carriages by the enormous oaks which grew so thickly on either side of the long drive that they shut out all sight of the rest of the estate, did nothing to lighten April's despondent mood. Nor did the sight of the imposing mansion before which they at last drew rein. The ivy-covered gray stone edifice with its numerous turrets and myriad of blank windows which seemed to frown down at them seemed to be warning her to keep away; telling her that she did not belong here. Yet, from their satisfied expressions as they looked about them at this evidence of luxury, this was where Edward and Beatrix thought she should be.

She felt something akin to panic. What ought she to do? She did not wish to enter this house, but if she begged them to allow her to go back to London at once, to forget about meeting her grandfather, would they listen to her? She thought they would not.

Beatrix attempted to persuade her brother to remain in the carriage until the great doors were opened to them. "You must remember who you are," she advised him. "Such a display is beneath your dignity as the husband of Lord Hannaford's heiress."

This time, however, Edward refused to listen to her advice. He was much too impatient to wait for one of his servants to make their arrival known.

"No, Bea," he exclaimed, his eagerness showing his wife how little attention she would have received from him if she had requested that they return home. "This is our future. And April's, too, of course. I have already waited far too long for this moment."

He sprang down from the carriage and rapped smartly upon the door with his cane, informing the footman who opened to him that he required to have immediate speech with the Earl of Hannaford. To what he considered to be an impertinent question from the servant concerning what sort of business he might have with the earl, he stated, "My name is Ainsworth."

"Yes, sir?"

Indignant, he stated, "You will inform his lordship that I have come to bring him his granddaughter, as I informed him that I should do."

The servant stared at him for a moment, as if he had been addressed in a foreign tongue, then turned to convey the message to a dignified butler who had approached by this time.

"His lordship has no granddaughter," that individual informed him, in a tone which brooked no denial. The footman looked as if he would have shrugged, had the butler not been watching him, then turned a blank face toward the caller and repeated the message.

He found himself, however, faced with one who was more determined than any number of servants could be. "I have already told you that my name is Ainsworth, fellow, and—as I had written to his lordship—I have brought the young lady home from France," Edward said sharply, "and I do not intend to stand out here all day and argue the matter with inferiors."

Feeling that greater authority was needed in this case, the butler stepped to the side of the footman who held the door.

"As you have been informed, sir, Lord Hannaford has no granddaughter. The members of this household are aware of that fact. Therefore, I suggest that you should take your leave." He made a sign to the servant to close the door upon the intruder, but Edward thrust himself forward, so that it could not be done.

"My wife is the daughter of Arthur Graves, Viscount Comber and his lady," he said, his temper rising with every delay, "and I have brought her here to her grandfather; since her parents' death, her place is here with him. Now, are you going to conduct us to the earl with no more procrastination, or must I instruct my servants to move you out of my path?"

"That will not be necessary— even if it were possible for you to do such a thing. You must see that you are quite outnumbered here." The insolent tone came from a fair-haired young man who had entered the hall in time to hear the last speech.

In contrast to the soft footsteps of the servants, the heels of his riding boots clicked upon the marble floor of the hall as he came to the butler's side to look down at the caller. He was dressed in buckskin breeches and riding coat which, although well worn, bespoke the mark of an excellent tailor, and he tapped a crop against his boot as he spoke, as if longing for an opportunity to use it.

Looking from Edward's cortege to the larger number of footmen who had silently appeared behind him in the hallway, quite as if they were expecting to be called upon to back up his words, the young man showed his teeth in an expression more like the anticipatory grin of a hungry shark than a smile of welcome. "However, Wilcox, I am certain you will find that my uncle will be only too eager to see the young—in the absence of a better term, shall we call her a lady?—who presumes to name herself his granddaughter."

"If you say so, Mr. Graves," Wilcox replied with some reluctance. He had been prepared to send this interloper packing and did not approve of having his wishes set aside by anyone, even the young gentleman. In the absence, however, of differing orders from the earl, he had no choice but to do as he was bid. Turning to Edward, he said, "If you and your—wife—will come with me, I shall announce you to His Lordship."

With a glance at April, which warned her to wait until she was summoned, Beatrix descended from the carriage. Mr. Graves stared at her opulent figure, one blond eyebrow nearly disappearing into his hair. "I beg of you, sir—" His tone conveyed more than a hint of doubtfulness that these callers deserved the least respect. "I believe you told the servants that your name is Ainsworth. I beg you not to expect that you will be able to convince anyone that my cousin had set up his nursery long enough ago to have been *this* female's father. I know he had not done so until, at the most, twenty-two years ago, and she must be at least the age he was when he died last year."

Beatrix shot him a murderous glance, and Edward said in a stiff tone, "This, sir, is my sister, Beatrix Ainsworth, if it is any of your affair. My wife is still in the carriage." Returning to the vehicle, he held out his hand and assisted her out. "Come, April. There is no need for you to fear this rude person, whoever *he* may be. I am certain your grandfather will give you a proper welcome."

"By all means, my lady, do come in at once," the young man said, bowing to April, the courtesy belied by his mocking tone. "I cannot wait to watch you as you attempt to face down my uncle. I hope you have been well trained in your lines."

April flinched at his disparaging words and drew closer to Edward, who put a comforting arm about her, scowling at the other man. "My wife has recently been ill," he said, "and can do well enough without being forced to listen to the slurs of a boorish farmer."

"Farmer? Do you intend that term for me? That remark demonstrates how little you know about the household, for all your claims to belong here, sir." Once more, the "sir" was emphasized in a manner which implied it was undeserved.

During this exchange of insults, the butler, having dismissed the curious footmen with a nod, had waited halfway down the hall. As Mr. Graves and the trio of newcomers neared him, he rapped lightly upon a door. In answer to a gruff summons, he opened the door and announced, "There is a gentleman here, Your Lordship, who says he has brought your granddaughter."

"My—I have no granddaughter, Wilcox, as you know quite well."

"That is what I took the liberty of informing him, my lord. However, Mr. Graves appears to think you might wish to speak with him and with the young person who has accompanied him."

"Oh, he did? It appears to me that my nephew takes a great deal upon himself at times. Still, I suppose I may as well see them, if that is what he thinks. But they should be warned that I shall have the pair of them behind bars if they cannot prove their story."

"Which, of course, they cannot do, Uncle, as you well know," Mr. Graves declared, preceding the callers into the room. "Arthur certainly never had a daughter, as it seems they intend to claim. I doubt they would have made such a showing as they have done to bring you a young female who was descended from some by-blow of yours. Or perhaps that is what they meant, and I misunderstood the—gentleman—for I thought he said that she was Arthur's daughter."

The old man gave a bark of laughter, not in the least displeased by the impertinence of the remark and said, "That will be enough from you, young jackanapes. Who told you I had any by-blows to have descendents?"

The eyebrow was raised again. "Now, Uncle—certainly you are not trying to tell me—"

"Never mind, never mind," the elder gentleman said, with a grin. "That is neither here nor there. We must permit them to tell their tale, I suppose, before we throw them out, since they have taken such trouble to prepare it."

"Hardly trouble enough to be accurate, I should say. Or perhaps they meant to say a by-blow of Arthur's," the younger man continued irrepressibly.

"I doubt that, I doubt that. As you say, that would scarcely be worth their trouble, for whatever claim she might have thought she had upon Arthur, she could not expect me to honor it. And who might *you* be?" he demanded, as Beatrix entered the room.

"This is my sister, Beatrix Ainsworth," Edward said. "I am Edward Ainsworth and this," he pushed April forward, "is my wife—your granddaughter. She is the former April Graves, *legitimate*," he cast an angry look at the other man, "daughter of your son. I wrote you as soon as we arrived in London that I was bringing her to you."

The Earl of Hannaford was a large man, taller than his nephew. He quite dwarfed Edward. When he rose to his feet and towered over April, she was more frightened of him than she had been of the younger man. "*Are* you my granddaughter?" the earl demanded in a tone fearsome enough to throw her into a panic.

"I—I do not—know, Your—Lord Hannaford." She could scarcely manage the words. "Edward has—has told me that I am."

"What does she mean—saying she does not know? Either she is Arthur's daughter or she is not." April had not thought he could sound more threatening than before, but he did.

"Not, of course. But you have startled her so greatly, Uncle, that she has forgot her lines. You should not bellow at her in such a way, but should tell her soothingly that she is facing prison for her imposture," Graves answered smugly.

"I warn you, sir—" Edward began.

Mr. Graves ignored the interruption. "Of course, they had to choose a young female to play the part—the older one would have convinced no one, unless she is pretending to be one of Arthur's particulars—but they need not have taken this shatterbrain."

"Will you keep out of this matter?" Edward snarled at the young man, his temper fraying at the constant gibes. "It has nothing whatsoever to do with you."

"How mistaken you are, Mr.—you did say your name is Ainsworth, did you not? It has everything to do with me. I think you may have missed my name—Alan Graves. Instead of being the boorish farmer you recently labeled me, I am Lord Hannaford's heir."

"Heir?" The word came from both Edward and Beatrix.

Beatrix said in scornful tones, "Of course. That is why he is objecting so strongly to our arrival. He knows that April's appearance means the loss of the inheritance on which he has been counting."

"Quiet, the lot of you!" The earl's tone was not to be denied, making April shrink away from him, as if fearing to be struck down. "This is not a tavern for the lot of you to brawl in. You are my heir, certainly, Alan, so far as my title and the entailed estate are concerned. Nothing can alter that, as we all know. But there are a number of other properties, as well. If there is any chance that this girl *does* prove to be Arthur's daughter—"

"Which she is not, of course."

"Be quiet, I told you. You do not know everything, although you may think that you do. Arthur and Elaine did have a daughter."

"This is the first time I have been told of such a daughter." There was scepticism in the young man's tone, as if he suspected his uncle of participating in a plot against him.

"Why should you have done?"

"Well, after all—a cousin—"

"I saw her only once," the earl continued. "That was a number of years ago, when they paid me a visit before the three of them took off on their travels. I think you were still only a schoolboy at that time, so you may be excused for knowing nothing about the girl. But she died in the same epidemic which took her parents in Paris, so the estate is not affected." He sank into his chair and fumbled with a paper knife, as if he might be ashamed to show any emotion at the thought of his son's and granddaughter's deaths.

"She did not die, Lord Hannaford," Edward put in. "In fact, she escaped the illness entirely, although she was the only one in the household to be so fortunate. I was in Paris at that time, and being Arthur's friend I promised him that I would bring his daughter to you, as I have done."

"If what you are telling me is the truth, why does the girl say she does not know whether she is my granddaughter or not?" the earl wanted to know. "I should not be able to recognize her, of course, since she was only a small child at the time I saw her, and would have changed greatly as she grew older. But the years have not made so great a change in me as that, except that my hair is white now. She would certainly know me."

"She would do so, I can assure you—if it had not been for her accident. Not more than a fortnight ago, April was badly injured when the carriage in which she was riding was overturned. She was thrown out of the vehicle, struck her head, and has lost her memory. The doctor assures me it will return in time, but for the moment, she knows nothing at all about her past."

Alan Graves clapped his palms together slowly three times, the gesture quite as derisory as the tone in which he exclaimed, "Oh, capital. You are proving far more ingenious than I thought you would be when I first saw you. So often, chicanerists—if I may be allowed coin a word—trip themselves up by making an error about some small point they ought to have remembered. But by planning in this way, if the chit should forget her lines, all she needs to say is that her memory was taken away in the accident."

April stared at him, biting hard upon her lower lip so that no one could notice its trembling. Up until now, everyone had been so kind to her since her accident. It was true, of course, that Beatrix was often impatient about matters for some reason April could not understand, unless if was out of jealousy because Edward seemed to like her. But not even Beatrix at her worst had been so scornful of her as this young gentleman. What had she done that he should be so cruel to her, except to be alive? Did he blame her for that? Tears welled into her eyes.

Alan felt a brief twinge of pity as he observed the girl's tears, but put it down at once. Of course, she would have to seem the injured innocent; that was her role. And he owned she appeared to be exceptionally good at it. Good enough to impress even him—for an instant. And she was quite attractive. But when the truth was told, she was no better than her accomplices. All three of them were determined to take away a part of the inheritance on which he had counted since he had been told of his cousin's death.

He would fight them every step of the way. And he would win. They might be able to gammon a soft-hearted old man—not that he had observed any signs of softness in his uncle until this moment—but having just been presented with the granddaughter he thought had died might well be enough to turn the earl's head.

However, *he* was not a sentimental fool to be taken in so easily by such a wild tale. If there had truly been a daughter, and he must own that his uncle should certainly know that much about Arthur's life, even if he did not, Hannaford must be shown that this could not be the same girl, that these people were no more than a trio of imposters—no matter to what lengths he was forced to go to convince the old man.

Beatrix had recognized Alan at once as an enemy. She moved to April's side and slipped an arm about her, much to the younger girl's surprise. The look which Beatrix gave the young man said, as plainly as words, "Do your worst. The game is ours."

Edward had ceased to pay the slightest attention to the other young man's comments, aware that his important task lay in convincing the earl of the truth of his statements, not in appeasing another claimant. Surely, Lord Hannaford's nephew would object to their presence at Silver Acres. He had considered himself to be his lordship's only heir. Now he was of no real consequence and could be ignored. As he had done in the doctor's office, Edward produced the papers which proved the death of the viscount and viscountess, and his subsequent marriage to their daughter.

Lord Hannaford examined them closely. "You say that you wrote, telling me that you were bringing the girl. I never received such a message."

"Doubtless it was to *someone's* advantage to see that it did not reach you," Beatrix said nastily. Edward frowned at her, warning her to say no more, but Mr. Graves merely gave a derisive snort.

"Had it arrived here, I should have seen it, Madam," the earl said in a tone with which not even Beatrix would have dared to disagree. "No one at Silver Acres has access to the post until I have finished with it. But we all know that messages do go astray at times, so the fact that it did not come to me means naught. These papers appear to be authentic," he said at last.

"Forgeries! You know they must be forgeries!" Alan howled. He tried to grasp the papers, intending to tear them to shreds, but his uncle held them tightly, just out of his nephew's reach.

"I said *appear*," he said. "I am not the one to say for certain, but I have friends who can find the truth for me in Paris, even in these times."

"Naturally, I shall expect you to verify what I have said," Edward agreed. "After all, you have only my word for what has happened—until such time as April regains her memory."

"And how long do you expect it to take for that to happen?" Alan asked sarcastically. "One would think you could have taught her her lines before you arrived, so that she could fling herself into my uncle's arms at once and claim him as her grandfather, rather than having to depend upon her fictitious loss of memory. I withdraw what I said about you earlier. You are not a well-organized group of knaves, after all."

Edward's fists clenched, but he said, "Naturally, you resent the fact that we are here, and I expect your insults. Expect them and discount them. They cannot do us any harm, since I have the proofs of April's right to be here. I do, however, resent your constant slurs against my wife."

"I say only what any thinking person would say under these circumstances."

"You are mistaken about that. Still, for me to fight you, as you apparently would like for me to do, would prove nothing at all, since you obviously have the advantage of size and appear to be well-accustomed to brawling, which I am not. And even if it were possible for me to best you, it could count for nothing, for this is not a matter which will be decided by fisticuffs but by legal proof. It is quite understandable that you should not wish to give up anything you thought was to be yours, but—"

"No, do not fight him, Edward," Beatrix ordered. "One has only to look at his behavior to see who is the knave here."

"You take advantage of your petticoats, Madam," Alan said furiously. "Knowing I cannot thrash you as I should like. In fact, the three of you should be whipped at a cart's tail."

"Be quiet!" The earl's roar set the window panes to rattling, and made the servants, who had drawn back into the hall in an attempt to learn what was happening, scurry to their posts, while April cringed away from him even more than before. "You take entirely too much upon yourself, Alan, to condemn these people without offering the slightest proof that they are not what they say. You are not master here yet, nor will you be for some time. Another such outburst as that, and I shall have you kicked off Silver Acres. Do you understand me?"

Alan Graves bit his lower lip between his teeth until it bled, as he nodded acceptance of his uncle's order. No matter what his personal feelings might be, he could not afford to be sent away from here—not now. How could he combat these three, fight for what had long been promised to him, if he were not on the premises?

He consoled himself with the thought that his uncle would certainly place the documents in his safe overnight. He had learned how to open that safe the first week of his stay here. There was nothing wrong in his learning about that, he told himself at the time; everything at Silver Acres, including the safe and its contents, would be his one day.

There had been no reason for him to make use of that knowledge—until now. Once the papers were in his hands, he would destroy them so not a shred was left; then let the cheats *try* to prove their tale.

For the moment, however, he had no choice but to accept his uncle's ruling and say no more. "I am certain you will excuse me, Uncle," he said stiffly. "Since you have made up your mind to accept these people, there is nothing more I can do here."

"Nothing at all," Beatrix said so softly that only April and Edward could hear her. The look she cast after the departing young man boded no good for his hopes of defeating them. True, it was that whey-faced little chit, April, who would be the old man's heiress—but April would need her husband to manage her affairs. And Beatrix knew how well *she* could manage Edward.

Chapter Six

To April, it appeared that everything about the estate of Silver Acres had been designed for the express purpose of daunting her—the size of the mansion and the great expanse of farms and woodlands which surrounded it, of which she so far had seen only the smallest part, the powerful old man who, according to the documents Edward had brought with them, was her grandfather, and most of all, Mr. Alan Graves. From the moment the three of them had arrived at the front door, he had declared himself her enemy, mocking her for not being able to prove to them, of her own knowledge, that she was really April Ainsworth, and determined to see that she was sent away—although she was certain he would much prefer to see her imprisoned for her claim of being the earl's granddaughter.

"What this man thinks of me should not matter," she said to herself as she wandered across the wide terrace, pausing to run her fingers over one of the marble figures situated at intervals along the balcony, enjoying the sensation of the cool stone beneath her hand, before descending the steps to the velvet-smooth lawn. "I may not be able to remember even a single thing about my past, but after all, Edward has brought the proof that I am who he says I am." And the earl had appeared to accept the proofs of her past—conditionally. At least, he had not ordered them away, but was permitting them to stay until he had verified Edward's claim.

Edward had told him that was what they wished him to do, for they wished only to make certain she was accepted. It would have been much better, of course, if he and Beatrix had been willing to delay their journey a bit longer, giving her the opportunity to regain her memory before they had come here, so that she could speak for herself. Then she could have assured the earl that she truly was his granddaughter, and not the adventuress Mr. Graves had been so quick to label her.

Until she could tell them she remembered who she was, she could understand that there might be some reason for doubting that she was truly April, for thinking her story had been merely contrived to cheat Lord Hannaford. It was only the younger man, however, who seemed so certain that she was a cheat, but the sarcasm he vented upon her was enough to wound her.

Except for the criticism from Beatrix—which she had decided was nothing more than jealousy because Edward was pleasant to her—he was the only one to speak so harshly to her. He was unquestionably set upon driving her and the others away from here. April wondered if he could persuade his uncle to do just that. It would be so nice to be able to stay here, if it were not for his anger at her. Being unable to prove to the gentleman that he was mistaken about her was so discouraging.

"And what about Caroline?"

She did not realize that she had spoken aloud until a man's voice demanded, "Who is Caroline? What does she have to do with all of this?"

She had thought herself quite alone out here. Startled, she whirled about, to find that her fair-haired young enemy was standing in the shadow of one of the giant oaks which bordered the drive, studying her in a manner she found most disconcerting.

"I do not know," she owned.

"So you have forgot your lines again? Is that what is worrying you today?" he queried.

Leaning his shoulders against the massive trunk, Alan crossed one ankle over the over as he looked at her, his manner that of one inspecting some alien thing which had wandered onto the estate by accident. His voice had been contemptuous, as it usually was whenever he spoke solely to her. She had heard him speaking pleasantly enough to some of the servants, as well as to his uncle—her grandfather.

It was a pity that they could not be friends, for April felt she needed friends, especially in this awe-inspiring place. She could understand that her coming must have meant some loss to him, but certainly so great an estate as this could provide for both of them, and much more. Also, Edward had said this was the largest of many estates owned by the earl. It seemed that the young man must be quite greedy to begrudge her even a small part of all this wealth, if it truly belonged to her.

"Really, my girl," he was continuing in that same tone, "you disappoint me by forever having to claim that you do not know this or that fact about your past life. Your—your husband—if that is who he is—should have drilled you in your role more thoroughly before you arrived, so that you could make a better showing."

"I think Caroline must be a friend of mine." She tried to ignore his repeated slurs at what he appeared to think was merely a pretended loss of memory, while she wondered why she was taking the trouble to give him any explanation about herself; he had no intention of believing her, whatever she might say.

Nonetheless, she plunged ahead. "Her name is the only thing I can remember from the time before the accident. Edward and Beatrix have told me they do not know anyone by that name. Still, they have promised to try to find her for me."

"A pity that she is not here at the moment, is it not? Perhaps she would be able to prove your tale to my uncle's satisfaction—and to mine, although I assure you that would

be a more difficult task. I am not an old man who has been
deprived of his only child, so I should not prove so gullible
as he, even if your missing friend came forward to verify
your tale."

"No, you would not believe it, whatever was said." The
words were said beneath her breath, since she was aware
he would merely laugh at her if she said them aloud.

"Or," he went on, "it might be that, if she does exist,
she is being kept from our sight because her words might
prove you to be an adventuress. Are you worrying that she
might appear and overset all your schemes?"

Stung at last to fury by the unfairness of his remarks,
April cried, "Why do you enjoy being so cruel? For you
must get much enjoyment from it, or you would not be as
you are. I must take criticism from Beatrix because she
knows everything and becomes impatient with me whenever
I cannot remember as she thinks I ought to do, despite the
fact that the doctor told us my recovery might take some
time. But there is no reason why I must stay here and listen
to more of your unkind accusations!"

She hurried away so that he might not see her tears. Tears
of anger as well as unhappiness. Everyone else at Silver
Acres had treated her most kindly, especially since they had
learned the story of her accident. Only this one man was
always cruel, baiting her whenever they met, accusing her
of being a thief and imposter.

"I do not want any of his money," she said beneath her
breath. "Not one penny of it. And I should like to tell him
so. All I wish is that I might be allowed to remain here and
be happy. I could be happy here, I am certain, as soon as
I am able to remember everything."

Whatever she might wish to do about her inheritance, however, she was even more certain that Edward and Beatrix—
but especially Beatrix—were anxious for Lord Hannaford
to make his announcement that she was his heiress. They
would never permit her to renounce the money.

Alan Graves whistled softly as he looked after the fleeing
figure. So the little adventuress had some spirit after all, did
she? Until now, she had been so quiet that he had thought

that she was ruled completely by the other two conspirators.

Perhaps he had been going about the task of proving their guilt in the wrong way, had made a mistake to speak to her as he had done. It might prove to be to his advantage to be nicer to the chit. Would she become too suspicious if he suddenly began treating her pleasantly? He did not think she would be, for her words made him believe she wished to have a friend.

Spirited or not, she was clearly the weakest link in the plot—if it was a plot, as he was certain it must be—and could doubtless be persuaded to tell him what he wished to know if he took the pains to handle her properly.

"After all, my lad," he reminded himself, "you are not entirely inexperienced in the art of bringing females around your thumb." He grinned at some of the memories evoked by the words, then frowned as he brought himself back to the present.

He now blamed himself for having been much too hasty in condemning her openly, both at their first meeting and again today. He had made her angry, which was what he had planned to do, of course, but which meant she would be all the more determined to tell him nothing which could be of help to him. It would have been better for him to have bided his time until he could prove his accusations, but he had allowed his quick temper to overcome his wisdom at the thought of being bilked of some of his inheritance.

He must go more slowly in his dealings with her, being a bit nicer at first, then beginning to show friendship. It should certainly serve his purpose to do so. She could never be persuaded to cooperate if he continued to accuse her of being an adventuress. Why should she do so, after all, when it meant she would be condemning herself?

On the other hand, he did not feel that she was nearly as clever as the older woman. It would do him no good to pretend a friendship with that one, for he suspected she could see through any such pretense. However, if he pretended that he was willing to be friends with the young chit, he had no doubt she could soon be induced to reveal the group's secret plans.

Once he had her admission that this was nothing more
than a scheme to get his uncle's money, he would be able
to expose her and her companions to the old man. When
he knew the truth about them, the earl would have them
imprisoned as he had threatened, or at the very least, would
order them off the estate. To see them sent to prison for
fraud would be preferable, of course, but it truly made little
difference to Alan which fate they earned, as long as they
were out of his life.

Unhappily, Alan had not yet been able to get his hands on
the papers the man Ainsworth had produced. His uncle had
kept them too close, not even placing them in the safe.

He had looked for them several times during the past few
nights without success. It seemed that they were nowhere
in the study or the library. Could it be that the old man suspected that his nephew had learned the secret of opening the
safe, and to prevent the papers from falling into his hands,
had kept them elsewhere?

Still, it would doubtless take some time for the earl to
begin any investigation of their story. Communications with
France were most uncertain at this time, and he believed
that his uncle's man had not been heard from recently. It
was quite possible that, being found to be in communication
with England, he had been condemned to the guillotine like
so many others.

"And without his help, it will be impossible for the old
man to have the papers verified," he said to himself. "Not
that there is a chance that they will prove to be anything
but forgeries."

It was always possible, however, that certain people in
France could be bribed to say they were genuine. After all,
what did he know about the trustworthiness of his uncle's
"man in France"? Even he could be one of the conspirators—assuming he were still alive. Of all his uncle's asso-
ciates, he would be the one who could have provided the
most information about Arthur and his family.

It was best to be safe, and if he could get his hands upon
the documents, it did not matter what claims the pair—he
should have said "the trio"—might make. Until he had been

able to do that, it might be the wisest choice to be kinder to the young woman.

Rather than fleeing to the house, where she might well have to face more of Beatrix' criticism, April had gone in another direction and soon found herself in the midst of an enormous rose garden. Determined to put the unpleasant Mr. Graves and his accusations out of her mind, she wandered for a time among the roses, admiring the variety of colors and sniffing their fragrance. Now and then, she bent to caress a blossom gently.

She wondered if she dared to cut some of them to take to her room, but had not seen any of the gardeners—she was certain it must take a small army of them to care for so large a place as this—and thought it unwise to take the blooms without permission.

She knew that she ought to return to the house and fetch a parasol, but she liked the feeling of the sunshine on her face, so remained where she was. Feeling soothed by the garden, she told herself that, at some other time, she would go over the house and study everything about it, for the glimpses she had of it made her certain it was filled with beautiful objects. There were paintings and carved furniture, as well as velvet drapes and marble mantelpieces.

Of course, she had not dared to go into a great many of the rooms, but had only peeped through the doors. "Beatrix would doubtless tell me I am being a fool to act as I do," she told herself. "She would say that, since this is my home, I have a right to go wherever I wish at Silver Acres. But do I truly have the right?"

Some day soon, she promised herself, she *would* see it all, even braving the wrath of Alan Graves to do so. "After all," she said aloud, "he does not own Silver Acres yet, so I suppose that I should have as much right to be here as he. That is what Edward and Beatrix have said, but I know the earl has not agreed that I belong here—yet."

She would prefer to see these beautiful things without the company of her husband or sister-in-law, for she felt that they were interested only in the value of the items they viewed. Of course, the house would belong at some time to Mr. Graves; but as long as her grandfather was alive, it was *he* who was master here, and if he approved of her, she might stay for a long time.

"With Edward and Beatrix, of course," she murmured with a sigh.

She wished sometimes that Beatrix would not plan to make her life with them, then dismissed that thought as a selfish one. It appeared that Beatrix had no other family than her brother, so it would not be the right thing to wish that she were elsewhere. Still, April could not help feeling resentful toward the older woman.

Edward was always kind to her in an absent-minded sort of way, and she was grateful to him for showing her that much consideration. It had been some days since she had thought he might have even the slightest interest in her as a female.

Their marriage was precisely what he had told her it was, merely a protection for her on the journey from France. She had no doubt, however, that Edward would always listen to Beatrix' opinions, which, as April sadly reminded herself, meant that *she,* too, would be kept beneath the older woman's thumb.

Once her memory had returned and she and Edward were truly living as husband and wife—as she supposed they would do in time, even if this had been merely a marriage of convenience—perhaps she could encourage him to make other arrangements for Beatrix. For the present however, although Edward and Beatrix appeared to be completely at home at Silver Acres, she could not help feeling somewhat out of place here.

"It is Mr. Graves who is responsible for my feeling as I do about the place," she told herself. "If it were not for him, I know I could accept Silver Acres as my home. But when he continually tells me I do not belong here, I begin to feel that it must be so—even though I know he is only saying that because he hopes I will go away and let him have all of grandfather's money."

It was indeed a pity that he felt about her as he did. If he did not make her so unhappy whenever they met, she believed she would have considered him quite good looking—as far as it was in her limited thoughts to judge. He was at least half a head taller than Edward, with broad shoulders and an erect carriage, set off by well-tailored clothing. He often wore riding clothes, and she thought nothing was more fitting for a man. His hair was fairer than her own and she thought his eyes were gray, although she had seldom looked closely enough at him to know if she was right.

In her opinion, much as it might be worth, he was a far more handsome man than Edward, although she supposed it was foolish, perhaps even wrong, of her to think so. After all, Edward was her husband—and Mr. Graves was the man who was attempting to prove her an adventuress. She ought not to approve of his appearance, or anything about him.

Lucy—she must remember to call the girl Martin, as it annoyed Beatrix to hear her say "Lucy"—came running to remind her that it was time for her to dress for tea. There was a flush to the girl's face which her mistress suspected had little to do with her haste.

"Why such urgency?" April asked.

"It—it is growing rather late."

"And you have been too occupied to notice the time?" her mistress teased. Lucy had caught the eye of a handsome young second footman when they arrived, and April was aware that she had slipped away several times to meet him since.

Lucy blushed and nodded, but April only laughed.

"It is a good thing that you, at least, can be happy here."

"Oh, I am certain you will be, too, when everything is settled. But you must change now, Madam. It *is* nearly time for tea."

April agreed and followed the servant into the house. There were times when she thought it was foolish beyond permission to have to change her gown half a dozen times a day. After all, there was no one else here to see what she wore, except Edward and Beatrix, both of whom were far more interested in the earl's property than they were in her. Still, Beatrix *had* gone to a great deal of trouble to find her the proper clothing for her meeting with her grandfather, so she supposed she ought to wear them.

"The only trouble with dressing to please him," April confided to her maid, "is that Grandfather seldom sees me. I know he is not strong, but I do not think my visits would overset him greatly. I should like to be able to talk with him more often, so that I could tell him how happy I am that I have such a nice home here."

"I think it is the young man who keeps you away much of the time. If he did not interfere, your grandfather would want to see you more often," Lucy observed.

"If that is so," April announced with sudden decision, "I shall go to see him today, whether Mr. Graves likes it or not."

Chapter Seven

"That is just what you should do," Lucy advised, knowing quite well that, had she spoken her mind so frankly to any other employer except Mrs. Ainsworth, she would be considered to be behaving impertinently. She would be facing a severe scolding if not dismissal for being so forward with another mistress.

In fact, at such times as this, when they were alone, Mrs. Ainsworth encouraged her to speak plainly about matters, even if they disagreed—which they did now and then. Had her mistress not also encouraged her to confide about her interest in the young footman? And how they had giggled together like a pair of children when she revealed that *his* name was also Edward! How Mr. Ainsworth would fume if he knew he shared his name with a common footman.

"Not at all common," Lucy had protested, sending the pair of them into giggles once more, as if they were small children at their games.

Beatrix would immediately have condemned her sister-in-law's attitude toward her servant if she had known of it, but April felt that Lucy's friendship had become more important to her since they had come here. Aside from the girl, she had no other friends, no one to whom she could turn.

Beatrix scolded her, Edward was busy with his attempts to convince the earl of her parentage, Mr. Graves mocked her, and she never had an opportunity to see her grandfather. She was far happier when she was gossiping with Lucy than at any other time.

"It is bad enough that you allow that old—I mean Miss Ainsworth," Lucy went on, "to dictate what you should do and what you should wear. There is no reason you should allow yourself to be ruled by your cousin."

"My cousin? Oh, I suppose that is what he is, even if he would be the last one to admit the relationship. I told him today that I did not like his endless fault finding. Not that I expect him to stop, merely because it displeases me."

"Good," Lucy agreed. "That is what the gentleman needs—someone to put him in his place."

"I could not agree with you more. But am I the one to do so?" April asked.

"Who has a better right to do so? After all, it is you who are the old man's granddaughter, are you not—and he is naught but a nephew."

"Naught but a nephew, you may call him, but, in truth, he is much more," April reminded her. "Since he is a man, he will be heir to Silver Acres—and who knows what more? Yet you may be right that he should be told of his faults and, as you say, I must be the one to do it, since I am certain no one else would attempt such a thing. Beatrix will tell him what she thinks of him, of course, but he pays no heed to her."

"Can you blame him for that?" the servant girl asked saucily, wishing that she had courage enough to defy the older lady. For all her sympathy with her young mistress, however, she quailed under Miss Ainsworth's criticism. And so did her mistress. It was not right, Lucy thought, but what could they do about it?

April giggled again at Lucy's question, thinking how nice it was to have someone with whom she could laugh over such matters. "No, I cannot—and I wish I could do the same. But I doubt if he would pay more heed to what I said, except to tell me I do not belong here. He does that so often that one would think he had the speech by heart. However, that is enough about that disagreeable man. I have decided—I intend to pay a call on my grandfather. And I shall go to him immediately—before I convince myself that I ought not to do so. Let me wear the rose gown."

"It will be just the thing for you."

"I think so, too. I know Beatrix does not like for me to wear it, but it is my favorite. I think my grandfather might approve of it. So would Edward if—" She stopped suddenly. How could she confide to a servant, even one she considered her good friend, that she thought her husband feared to disagree with his sister about anything?

Lucy Martin did not need to be told anything about that matter. She could hardly miss seeing how Edward Ainsworth deferred to his sister in every way, ignoring his wife's opinions—almost as if he were afraid to do otherwise. But why should a man fear his sister? Was he not the head of his family?

Or was it that he feared she might become so angry if he did not agree with whatever she wished that she might interfere with his plans for the young lady's reconciliation with her grandfather? It was doubtful that Miss Ainsworth would do anything of that kind, since she too would profit by the reconciliation. That was one thing her mistress had never mentioned, but there was gossip enough in the servant's hall about her reason for having come here.

Lucy reminded herself that she should not take a part in all of this, except that she sympathized with her young mistress. April's sudden decision to defy the older woman by wearing the rose-colored gown—and why should they have purchased, it, if it was to be hung away in the armoire?—made her smile as she hurried to bring out the gown and help April into it, then to arrange her hair.

"I suppose the old besom will say it is not done right," Lucy told herself as she surveyed her finished work. "But at least, it will give her something else to complain about, besides the rose-colored gown." Miss Ainsworth had not had the chance to summon a proper hairdresser to instruct

Lucy, so the girl was left to do her best. Her best, of course, was never good enough to please the older lady, but April was satisfied with the result.

Soft waves of fair hair hid the tiny scar from her injury. Lucy told herself that Mrs. Ainsworth had never looked better than she did at this moment. Her rose-colored gown seemed to reflect a bit of color onto her pale face, and her eyes gleamed with anticipation of her forbidden visit.

As she approached her grandfather's study, April met the butler coming along the hall. "How is my—His Lordship—feeling today?" she asked, wondering why it was so hard for her to claim him as her grandfather when she spoke to others.

"He is feeling stronger today, Miss—Madam." Wilcox corrected himself, slightly embarrassed by his lapse. It was difficult, however, for him to think of this little thing as a married woman.

"Then I think it would be a nice thing for me to call and bid him a good day." At his sudden frown, she asked, "He has not forbidden my visiting him, has he?"

"No—His Lordship has said nothing. At least, to me. But Mr. Graves—"

"Is Mr. Graves his physician?"

"Certainly not, Mi—"

"Call me miss if it pleases you to do so; I shall not mind. But I see no reason why I should abide by Mr. Graves' ruling about whether or not I should see my grandfather." There! She had said it. In one breath, she had claimed the older gentleman as her grandfather and defied the younger one to keep her from seeing him.

Wilcox permitted himself the slightest of smiles. "As you say, Miss April." The smile widened as she passed him and reached the study door. It had been Mr. Ainsworth of whom he had disapproved at their first encounter, not the young lady, and he wished her well in her meeting with his lordship.

Mr. Graves would be quite displeased when he learned that she had visited the old gentleman—but Mr. Graves was not master here yet. Nor would he be for some time; the old gentleman was stronger than he appeared and would not be sticking his spoon in the wall for many a year. And *he* had given no orders to exclude the young lady from his presence.

April rapped softly at the door and entered in response to a gruff invitation. The earl looked up from the paper he had been studying to ask, "And to what do I owe this visit, young woman?"

At least, he had not ordered her to leave, which she felt was a good sign. April swallowed nervously, and said, "I only wanted to wish you a good day and ask how you are feeling."

"This concern for my welfare is a bit sudden, is it not?"

Should she tell him that it had been Mr. Graves who had been preventing her from visiting him in the past? No, there was no reason why she should stir up any trouble between the two gentlemen. For all she knew, Mr. Graves might have been acting upon Lord Hannaford's orders when he informed the three of them that the earl's health did not permit him to have visitors. "I—I was not certain whether you would wish to see me."

He studied her for several moments, while she waited, twisting her handkerchief between her fingers, then smiled at her and motioned her to seat herself in a large chair near him. Happily, she sank into its soft leather-covered depths. When she saw his smile, she was no longer afraid of him. She could think of him as her grandfather; she might even be able to call him that when she spoke to others.

"Yes, I think I have wished very much to see you and speak with you, my dear," he said in a tone which was so far different from the one which she had found so frightening at their first meeting that it was difficult to recall why she had ever shrunk in fear of him. "It has been remiss of me not to invite you in before this. Tell me, child—have you remembered anything more about your earlier life?"

"No." She shook her head. "It worries me that I cannot do so. Although the doctor explained to us that sometimes it takes many weeks for one to recover from such an accident as mine, I wish I could remember something—anything—

of the past. Even one tiny thing that seemed familiar to me would help me to know I belong here."

"But you were so small when you were here last. You might well not remember anything about the place." That was, if she proved to be April. He had a feeling that she might be.

"I know—I know that is what you have told me. But I do not remember coming here at all, nor do I remember being in any other place, either. As it stands now, I sometimes have the oddest feeling that I did not exist at all until the day I woke in the doctor's surgery after the accident. I know it is foolish of me to feel as I do, but I cannot help it."

"Then you do not remember why you were running away from your husband?" he asked, placing a hand over hers. If the man was cruel to her in some way, he must see to it that she was fully protected from further persecution. He was forced to admit that he had not seen signs of such mistreatment, but after all, the man was certain to be on his best behavior when he was hopeful of seeing his wife inherit a great sum of money.

It might be the best thing, he said to himself, *if I were merely to settle the property and money on her at once, rather than making her wait until I die to inherit. As much as I should like to keep her with me, she and her husband might prefer a home of their own on one of the other estates. Especially if Alan continues to claim that she has no right to anything. It will not to do to have them constantly quarreling.*

Of course, the girl must truly prove to be Arthur's daughter; then she will inherit. My own feeling about her is not enough, because I am wishing it to be true. It is time I began to look into the matter.

He studied her face carefully, hoping he would be able to see at least a slight resemblance to his beloved late wife— that would have been enough to convince him, without need for checking her papers—but there was nothing he could recognize. She did not look at all like him, either, but he was happy for that; his were certainly not the proper assortment of features for a young female.

Nor could he find any resemblance to Arthur; doubtless, she was more like her mother. Having been in her company only a few times after she and Arthur were married, he could not recall much about the woman, save that she had been fair haired. As fair, perhaps, as this girl?

April had been silent for so long that he thought she had forgot his question, then said, "No—I cannot remember anything of that time, either. As I said, it is as if I had no life before I found myself in the surgery. But I cannot feel that I would have been running away from Edward. He is always so kind to me now." *When Beatrix is not around to interfere,* she added silently. "I am certain he must have been that way before I went away."

"Then, if you feel that way about him—as you should do—you have nothing to fret about."

"I suppose I do not, but I cannot help myself," April continued. "Edward and Beatrix tell me they think I may have been attempting to find my friend Caroline, but they say they do not know her. Nor do I know anything about her, except for her name, and this feeling I have that it is important for me to find her—that she needs my help."

The thought appeared to distress her, so the old man reassuringly patted the hand which lay beneath his. "I have heard your husband say that they are doing whatever they can to find your friend. She may not be in this country, my dear, since you have so lately come from France. That may be the reason you worry about her."

"Oh yes—that could be it. If that is where I left her—"

"Or perhaps she was a friend from your childhood, one you have not been seen since you have been traveling."

April nodded. "I suppose you are right." She still looked doubtful, however, making him wish he could say something to ease her unhappiness.

"You will remember, however, that I still have friends in France, so if she is there, it may be that I can help to find her for you." After he had assured himself that she was who she claimed to be—or rather, who Ainsworth claimed her to be.

"Oh, if you would do that, I should be so grateful, gr—Lord Hannaford." She felt that, although she might call him so to herself, she could not refer to him as "grandfather" to his face until he gave her permission to do so. Would that time ever come?

She hoped that it would come soon; it would be nice to know she belonged to someone. Of course, she belonged to Edward now—but that was something quite different. "You cannot know how distressing it is to have the name Caroline always in my mind, but to be unable to see her face or where she might be. As you say, she may be someone I left in France. I hope she is in no danger. So many people are in great trouble there, or so Edward has told me."

"I am certain she must be safe." If the other girl were still in France, he doubted for her safety, but would not overset the girl further by speaking of the possible dangers her friend might be facing. "I shall see if something can be done for her," he promised. "Now, my dear, I heard the bell ring to announce tea, so you had best run along. We shall speak again some other time."

"Are you not coming to tea?" She asked the question eagerly, thinking it would be pleasant to share the the meal with him, now that he was being so kind to her.

"No—I have matters to which I must attend, so Burrows will bring my tea to me here. If it were not that I would be preoccupied, I might ask you to stay and share it with me. But now that you have found the way, you must visit me often. No need for you to wait for an invitation."

"Oh, I shall do so—and thank you for asking me." She curtsied, then dared to blow a kiss toward him before leaving the room.

In the hall, she met Alan Graves, who demanded, "What were you doing in my uncle's study?" The thought that she had been visiting the old man in defiance of his wishes made him forget his plan of winning her friendship. Who knew what tales she might have been spinning to win his confidence?

"I was paying him a visit."

"But you were told—"

"I was told *by my grandfather* that I must come to see him quite often." What would he say to that?

Alan bit back the words he had intended to say. If she had got around the old gentleman to that extent, it would be best for him to move carefully until he could prove their trickery. It would not do to have her complaining to his uncle of his mistreatment of her. "I am happy that you had a pleasant visit."

"Oh yes, quite pleasant."

She moved past him, but he said, "By the way—"

"Yes?" She looked back at him, head tilted to one side.

"Oh—I merely wanted to say that you should always wear that color. It is most becoming."

She thanked him, looking puzzled. But no more puzzled than he, as his gaze followed her. Now why, he wondered, had he said that?

Chapter Eight

What he had said to her was true, of course; the rose gown had been quite becoming, and he had noticed before that she was a pretty little thing, regardless of what color she might be wearing. Still, he was soon able to convince himself that his only reason for paying her a compliment was his wish to overcome her reservations. That *had* been his plan, had it not?

"Of course that is all it was—something to win her confidence," he muttered. "A trick to counteract her many tricks." When he had convinced her that he preferred to be friends rather than enemies, it should not be difficult to get the truth from her.

How clever it had been of her to pay a visit to his uncle when no one else was about. He had not thought her capable of making such devious plans—or had the others told her what she ought to do? Her artless ways and her claim not to know who she truly was might be enough to convince the old man that she was who she pretended to be, but he continued to tell himself that *he* would never be convinced.

His arguments with himself were cut short by the sound of carriage wheels on the drive, and he approached the door as the footman threw it open to admit a young pair from the nearest estate.

"Alan, how wonderful it is to see you," the lady cried. "I hoped that you would be at home." Having been told by an admirer no longer remembered—except for his compliment—that her long eyelashes were one of her best features, she fluttered them at the gentleman. She had determined that before the end of summer, she would bring Alan up to scratch. After all, he would someday be the Earl of Hannaford, and she had visions of herself as a countess.

If her prey had any idea of what she had in mind, he gave no sign. "Virginia, Gilbert," he said, extending a hand to each. Looking from one of them to the other, he said, "May I guess what brings you here?" Actually, he had expected a visit from them before this.

The reason for the delay was soon explained. "We returned from a visit to our Scottish relatives," Gilbert explained, "and you can have no idea of how dreary such a visit could be—"

"To be greeted with the news that you, Alan, had unexpected guests," his sister interrupted.

"One of them, by all reports, a delectable morsel."

"Do be quiet, Gilly. The moment she heard, of course, nothing must do for Ma*ma* but that we should come and see for ourselves—that is, to report to her."

"Of course." The Viscountess Menton prided herself on being the first in the countryside to learn all the gossip. It was only surprising that she had not accompanied her children at this time.

"You know Ma*ma*," Gilbert said, shrugging. "Not that we objected to coming. Virgie has not seen you for nearly a month—"

"Gilly!" Virginia said menacingly, but the young man merely laughed.

"And when I heard of the little charmer, I thought it wise to come along. Let us see her at once—unless you feel that just because you saw her first—"

"Hardly that," Alan said with a laugh. He was not particularly amused, although he realized that the news of their unwanted visitors—unwanted, at least, by him—could hardly be kept from their neighbors. "Come into the drawing room and I can have Wilcox—ah, I see it will not be necessary. I should have known they would not be late for tea."

As usual, Beatrix and Edward led the way into the room, April slowly following them. She had not been aware of the newcomers, although Beatrix had known of them from the moment their carriage approached.

Ignoring the trio for the present, Alan said, "Wilcox, will you inform my uncle that we have guests?"

"I have done so, Mr. Graves, but His Lordship says he hopes they will excuse him, as he has some business he must finish."

"Very well." Since the moment could be delayed no longer, he turned from one group to the other. "May I present our neighbors—the Honorable Miss Virginia Soames and her brother, Gilbert Soames."

"Dash it, Graves, you might have said the *Honorable* Gilbert," the gentleman complained, brushing his moustache and ogling April, who stepped behind Edward.

"And our guests, Mr. and Mrs. Ainsworth, Miss Beatrix Ainsworth."

"It is so wonderful to have new faces among us," Virginia said, advancing toward Beatrix with an outstretched hand. "And may I say, Mrs. Ainsworth, that you certainly do not look old enough to have a grown daughter."

Alan shouted with laughter while Beatrix glared at the young lady, ignoring the outstretched hand. "I am *Miss* Ainsworth," she said cooly. "April is my brother's wife."

Gilbert's laugh was as loud as Alan's. "Trust Virgie to put her foot in it. For myself, may I say how happy it makes me to see all of you." His gaze, however, had not left April, who shifted uncomfortably and attempted to hide behind Edward. She did not know how to deal with so brash a young gentleman.

"My wife is Lord Hannaford's granddaughter, whom I have brought home from Paris," Edward announced. If the word was spread about the countryside, it might do much to hasten the earl's acceptance of April.

"So she claims, at least," Alan Graves said dryly. "It has yet to be proven."

The visitors would have commented on that, but Wilcox appeared at that moment to announce tea. Gilbert was more than willing to accept Alan's lukewarm invitation to remain, but Virginia tugged at his arm. The older lady was still glowering at her because of her *faux pas*, and it was evident that Virginia would not have a moment alone with Alan.

"No, I thank you, but we must go," she said. "Ma*ma* will be expecting us to tell her all about your visitors, and you know how testy she can be if she is kept waiting."

"I do, indeed." Even if Alan were as interested in the young lady as he knew she wished—and he certainly was not—he would have thought at least twice before taking on so formidable a mother-in-law. "But you will come again? And soon?"

"You may be certain of that," Virginia told him. "And it has been—interesting—to meet your guests."

"Insufferable chit," Beatrix commented as they made their way to the tea table.

"Oh, Virgie is merely thoughtless," Alan said, unable to keep back a smile as he recalled the young lady mistaking Beatrix for April's mother. *A mistake anyone might make given the sister's looks,* he thought. "And Gilbert, of course, is nothing but an unlicked cub."

Personally, he would enjoy giving the cub a few solid thwacks. *He* might assure himself that April was nothing but an adventuress, but to Gilbert, she was Ainsworth's wife and so should be beyond his unpleasing attentions. He was certain they *had* been unpleasing to the girl, and should have been so considered by her husband.

Alan's comments about the callers did nothing to endear him to Beatrix, as she recalled his laughter at her expense. He would soon have little to laugh about when Lord Hannaford acknowledged April.

The young man had no fear of such an event ever taking place. Ainsworth could bring out all the credentials in the world and Alan would still be certain the papers were forgeries and that they were a pair of adventurers. A trio, he should have said; the girl was clearly a part of it, although he was beginning to wonder about her.

Instead of being one of the original conspirators, had she perhaps been chosen by the man and woman to play the role merely because she might fit the description of the real April? In such a case, she might not have taken a part in devising this scheme to deprive him of a great part of his inheritance; but even if she had not been equally as deep in the conspiracy as her companions, she certainly should have learned enough by now of what the other two were planning to do.

And whatever she knows, I can persuade her to tell me what it is—if I can remember not to lose my temper and say something which will anger her again, he thought. It should not be too difficult to win her trust; all he needed to do was to flatter her now and then.

This April—for lack of any other name, he must think of her by that one, which he strongly doubted was her own—had colored quite prettily when he had commented upon her gown. He felt that Ainsworth, once having hired the chit, no longer felt it was necessary for him to say such things to her, if he had ever done so. And it was clear that she-wolf of a sister did whatever she could to keep the pair of them under her thumb.

He had already made the mistake of showing his opinion of them when they first arrived at Silver Acres, and the she-wolf had defied him on the spot to prove that they were the adventurers he knew them to be. She would remember that, even if the younger one did not, so she was the one he must beware of. He had been aware of that from the first day. It was the females who were always the more dangerous, whatever they undertook.

Even the ones who appeared innocent must be carefully watched, he warned himself. Especially those, for they could take a man off guard. However, he was still of the opinion that it was the older woman who was the brains behind the entire plot—if there was a plot.

Why did the thought that April might not be as culpable as he first thought come to his mind time after time—was it merely because the girl was not unpleasant to look at? He realized that he was becoming more confused about her role in this affair each time he met her, that there were times when he found himself almost liking the wench. It made no difference if he did so; he was still determined to prove that there *was* a plot to rob him of his rights, and that she was a part of it—whether she was willing or not.

A large sum of what he considered to be his rightful inheritance depended upon his being able to discredit them. If only he could find some way to get his hands on those papers his uncle was holding! They would be ashes in moments once he had them—and then, let the others *try* to prove their claim.

Since he had not yet been able to do so, his best hope of success was to win the girl's confidence. "Just a bit of flattery, properly applied, can do more than any number of gifts," he told himself. "At least, when given to this type of female. And I believe I can apply it as well as any other."

He would have to move carefully, of course, if he was to do so. Since she was Ainsworth's wife, or even if she had merely been hired to play such a part, he could not appear to admire her so openly that the husband would consider it proper to take offense at his actions. He knew how strongly his uncle would object to his doing anything of that sort.

He had already earned the old man's disapproval by his open scorn of the trio and their motives. No—rather, it had been because he refused to believe that his cousin had a daughter. At least, he had refused to believe *this* female could be the daughter. His belief on that point would not change, although he sometimes doubted that she was the conspirator he had first thought her.

If he gave the earl any further reason to take exception to his behavior—such as being accused of having made an attempt to attract the jade—he would be sent away from Silver Acres. Not permanently, perhaps—for his uncle was fond of him in his way—but at least for as long as they remained here. That could not be allowed to happen, for if he were not at hand, he would have no way of combating their scheme to take away what he had considered since his cousin's death to be his rightful property.

Knowing of the report the young Soameses would have carried home, no one in the family was surprised to see the viscountess' crested carriage arrive at Silver Acres early next day. Wilcox sent one of the footmen to tell the earl of her coming before he approached the door, and his lordship came from his study to await her. Leaning on her cane and upon the strong arm of her coachman, the tiny lady mounted the steps. Lord Hannaford came to her side and proffered his arm.

"Welcome to Silver Acres, Sybil," he told her. "It has been some time since we have been honored by a visit from you."

"These days, I sit at home and wait for people to come to me," she said, sinking into a chair and adjusting her wig, which had become disarranged as she alit from her carriage. This wig was the same raven hue as her daughter's hair, and looked odd above her wrinkled and painted countenance. Her friends, however, discounted this as one of her many foibles.

Taking a chair beside her, the earl said, "May I offer you a sherry, my dear?"

"Sherry! Namby-pamby drink. But I would not say no to a brandy."

"Certainly." Lord Hannaford turned to give the order, only to find Wilcox at his side, offering a tray with two glasses of the spirit. Her ladyship's tastes were no secret in the household.

After a hearty sip from her glass, Lady Menton said, "You know what brings me today, of course. Unless my stupid louts of children have it all wrong—as I do not doubt they have, for both of them have more hair than wit—your lost granddaughter has come home to you."

"She says that she is my granddaughter," Lord Hannaford responded. "That is, her husband says so, for the girl has apparently lost her memory due to an accident. He has papers to prove her claim, but I have not yet been able to verify them."

"Hah—a romance. And you have been keeping her from the countryside, I hear."

"They only arrived here a short time ago. April—if she truly is April—her husband and his sister."

"Yes, Gilly told me about Virginia mistaking the sister for the younger gel's mother." She took another sip of her brandy. "I can imagine how well that was received."

Hannaford laughed. "I did not hear it, but, having dealt with the woman, I doubt that Virgie created a bosom friend by that remark. Which is neither here nor there; one must receive her, since she is April's sister-in-law, but I find her common, as would you."

The viscountess tapped his arm with an admonitory finger. "Please allow me to judge for myself. You know I came today expressly to see the lot of them."

"Wilcox—"

"I have already taken the liberty, my lord, of informing your guests of Lady Menton's arrival." He had been in no doubt of the reason for her call.

"Does he always anticipate your wishes?" the viscountess asked, looking sharply at the butler's impassive face.

"Quite frequently," Lord Hannaford owned. "One becomes accustomed to it in time."

The Ainsworths arrived at that moment and were presented to her ladyship. Recalling that this was the mother of the young lady who had so insulted her yesterday, Beatrix was at first of the opinion that she should say something to the lady about her daughter's manners, then changed her mind and said instead in honeyed tones, "We are honored, Lady Menton. It is always such a good thing to meet friends of our dear April's grandfather."

"If he *is* her grandfather—a matter which is still very much in doubt," Alan Graves said, having entered the room in time to hear the last remark. He bowed over the viscountess' hand, raising it to his lips as he said, "I was certain we should have the honor of seeing you today."

"Go away, hedge-bird, I did not come to see you. You, gel," she beckoned to April. "Come closer. Let me look at you."

April approached somewhat timidly. Although the lady was even smaller than she, there was something about her which said that she expected to be obeyed.

After a long inspection which made April feel that the viscountess could see all the way to her bones, Lady Menton patted her hand and smiled. "Very pretty, my dear. I was about to say that you would take quickly, but I recall that you are already taken. Pity, in a way. But then . . . When do you give a ball to introduce her to all your friends, Hannaford?"

"I can scarcely present her to my friends until I have proved to my own satisfaction that she is my granddaughter."

"Nonsense! Why else would she be here?"

"I can think of a good many reasons," Alan said. "All of them golden."

"Oh yes—she will take something from you, will she not? No wonder *you* do not wish to acknowledge her. But Hannaford should not mind that. However, if you do not wish to give a ball for her, my lord, *I* shall do so."

"But not to present her as my granddaughter until that has been proven," added Lord Hannaford.

"What difference should that make to me? I shall give it in honor of your visitors—all of them. And now that is decided, I must take my leave." Rising with difficulty, she waved aside any effort to help her, and made her way out to her carriage, leaving her listeners staring after her.

Chapter Nine

When Lady Menton made up her mind about a subject, there was no gainsaying her. Within the next several days, her servants were driven nearly to distraction by the many orders she gave them to prepare for her ball.

The country was naturally rather slim of company at this time of year, because many families preferred to do their visiting now. However, there were still enough neighbors to make a respectable crowd. Footmen were sent out in every direction, bearing invitations, while the household servants polished the already immaculate rooms and prepared a feast to satisfy at least twice the number of guests who could be expected to come. Everyone within miles was more than eager to attend any festivity given by her ladyship.

With one exception.

"I shall not attend," Alan declared when the invitation reached Silver Acres. "Our presence at this affair will make it seem that we approve of these imposters, and I, for one, will not do so."

"You will go," his uncle told him. "What you may think of the Ainsworths has nothing to do with the matter. They may be telling the truth or they may not. But Sybil Menton is a friend of many years, and no one living beneath my roof is going to insult her by refusing to attend her ball."

For an instant, the younger man was angry enough to retort that he would leave Silver Acres before he would take a part in this affair, then reminded himself that nothing would better suit the Ainsworths—especially Beatrix—than for him to leave the field to them. Reluctantly, he acceded to his uncle's order.

He could not know it, but April was nearly as reluctant to go as he. "There will be so many people," she confided to Lucy, "and all of them strangers to me. I know I shall be terrified of meeting them."

"But you know that everyone is a stranger to you now," the girl told her. "So this will be no different. And at least, you have met Miss Soames and her brother."

"Yes—I own that I did find her quite pleasant, the few moments we spent together. But I am not so certain that I wish to meet her brother again."

"Oh, he can do nothing to harm you at a ball. Besides, ma'am, it might be that there will be things that will help you to remember. You told me the doctor said anything might do that."

"That is true," April said slowly. "It might be of help. But, unless my memory does return, I shall not know how to dance."

"That should not worry you," Lucy said. "Once you have seen it done, you will be able to follow the steps. And your ball gown is so beautiful."

April could not argue about that. The gown was exactly what she would have chosen for herself, and she was surprised that Beatrix had allowed the couturiere to have her way in the matter. It was made of deep green satin, the draped overskirt of sea-green net, with bandings of the same pale color at the neckline and the edge of the puffed sleeves. Her velvet mantle was of the same deep green as the body of the gown. Once she had donned it, April felt that, at least, she *looked* as if she was the earl's granddaughter, and that she might be able to endure the evening after all.

Her courage wavered when she saw the crowd of guests assembled in Lady Menton's rooms, but her ladyship, garbed in startling scarlet and with a wig of bright golden curls, came to welcome them as if they were all close friends. Since the viscountess' invitations had read that the ball was given in honor of the earl's visitors—with no mention of April's possible relationship to the old man, as she had promised—the newcomers soon found themselves amid those wishing to make them welcome. If Lord Hannaford and Lady Menton accepted them, the others were quick to follow their example.

Unlike many such affairs, the young ladies among the guests were outnumbered by the gentlemen, so both April and Beatrix found themselves besieged by dancing partners. April was shy at first of agreeing to dance, but found that she had no trouble in following her partners' steps, and she was passed from one flattering young gentleman to another. She thought they should have asked Edward's permission to dance with her, but decided that it was possible that more freedom might be permitted at such affairs than she would expect.

Beatrix was at first inclined to resent the way the young gentlemen swarmed about April, but when she began to receive the same attention from a number of important gentlemen—if not such young ones as her sister-in-law appeared to be attracting—she entered into the spirit of the evening. She was careful, however, to remark to each of her partners that April was the earl's granddaughter. She had heard Lady Menton promise Hannaford that *she* would not do so, but even her hostess could not complain if one of her guests mentioned the fact.

Seeing that both the ladies from Silver Acres were well attended, Lady Menton looked about to find partners for Mr. Ainsworth. However, he appeared to be better pleased to stand about talking with some of the older gentlemen. As Beatrix was doing, he was acquainting them with his wife's relationship to Lord Hannaford.

His lordship had retired to the card room with several of his cronies, which the viscountess thought was no more than could be expected. By doing so, he need not openly own the girl as his granddaughter, but neither did he deny it. Alan Graves had danced with several of the young ladies, but Lady Menton frowned when she saw that her daughter was clearly coaxing him to dance with her a second time. Even a London Season, it seemed, had not been enough to teach the girl to be more subtle in her approach. Young gentlemen did not like to be pursued. If Virginia made herself the object of talk, word was certain to be carried back to London next Season, and her chances of bringing young Graves or anyone else up to scratch would be lost.

Her ladyship made her way to her daughter's side, taking care to step upon the edge of her gown. "Dear me, Virgie," she said in mock penitence, "I fear I have torn your flounce. You must go and pin it up at once."

Virginia gave her mother an angry glance, but dared not disobey, so went off to pin up the non-existent tear. Alan gave the viscountess a look of gratitude, which soon changed as she said, "Young man, I have seen that you have not yet danced once with your cousin."

"I beg Your Ladyship's pardon, but the—but she is *not* my cousin."

"Well, that is neither here nor there. She is a guest in your uncle's house, and that is reason enough for you to lead her out for a dance."

"I am certain she does not lack for partners." In fact, he could have named every young puppy who had danced with her.

"That may be, but the fact that you pointedly refrain from approaching her is certain to be noticed by everyone. It is insulting to the gel, whoever she may be." She drew herself to her full height, reaching little more than to his shoulder. "Now, are you going to march over there and ask her to dance with you—or must I take you by the ear and lead you to her?"

Alan laughed as he looked down at the formidable little lady. "I believe you would do exactly that," he told her. "Very well, cousin or not—and I *know* she cannot be—I shall do as you say."

As he started, still reluctantly, toward the crowd of young gentlemen surrounding April, he saw that Gilbert Soames seemed to be urging her to accompany him onto the floor. "But I cannot do so," he heard her protest. "I have already danced with you once—"

"A country dance," he argued. "This is a waltz."

"But it is a second dance—"

"Rather than threatening me, Lady Menton would do well to teach that gudgeon of a son of hers some manners," Alan said beneath his breath, hastening his steps toward them.

"This is our dance, I believe," he said aloud, moving around Gilbert to slip an arm about April and lead her onto the floor for the waltz.

Startled by his unexpected arrival, April stumbled over his feet several times before she was caught up in the rhythm of the dance. "Th-thank you for coming to my rescue," she said. "I did not know what to do—he was so insistent—"

"Certainly you should know how to handle a man," he told her.

"But I do not. Or if I ever did so, it is something I cannot remember."

"Ah yes—that convenient memory of yours. I keep forgetting how well you use it."

"I—do not know what you mean," April replied.

"Dancing, for example. How does it happen that you can remember that, if you have forgot everything else?"

"I did not remember—but once I began to dance, it was as if I had done so before. Lucy told me it would be this way."

"Who is Lucy? Another of your mysterious friends, like this Caroline?" Alan smiled.

"Lucy is my maid. I do not know about Caroline, except that I worry about her." She pulled as far away as the circle of his arms would permit, to ask, "Why did you come to dance with me, if all you intend to do is quarrel?"

He could scarcely tell her that he had been ordered to do so by a lady so tiny he could have tucked her under his arm. "I—thought perhaps you would find me preferable to young Soames."

"I should do, if you would not always be so quarrelsome. You dance much better than he. And I do not like his moustache."

Alan was forced to laugh. "Poor Gilly. He has spent so much time trying to raise a respectable moustache, and gives it quite as much attention as he does to his cravat."

"I cannot say that I like that, either." Alan's cravat was much neater, she thought. In fact, she had thought all evening that he was quite the handsomest man in the place. It was no wonder that Virginia Soames was making a fool of herself over him.

Alan laughed again. "Then, at least, we have found one thing on which we agree. Gilbert is quite beneath our notice—so we shall ignore him for the rest of the evening." This might be a good time to begin his plan for capturing her interest. "Let me take you down to supper," he suggested, "and then dance with me again."

"But two dances—" Somehow, although she was not certain how, she knew that such an action was most improper.

"You are a guest at Silver Acres—that will make it quite all right," Alan reassured her.

"You are certain of that?"

"Quite certain. And think what that will do to Gilly's self-esteem."

"In that case," April told him, laughing, "I shall be happy to do so."

From the center of her own band of admirers, Beatrix watched the pair of them laughing together. So the wretch was exerting himself to please April and, from all appearances, succeeding all too well. Who knew what she might tell him? Why was Edward not watching her to see that she was not confiding her life's history to the villain?

Then she began to chuckle. How could April say anything beyond what they had already told the earl? She could not remember what had happened, had no idea where she had been going at the time of the accident. Let Mr. Graves waste his time being nice to her. He would sing a different tune when Hannaford acknowledged his granddaughter openly.

The fact that he had been willing to bring the three of them to this ball meant that full acknowledgment was merely a step away.

That evening, long after the Ainsworths were sleeping, Alan Graves sat in his room, gazing across the moonlit lawns of Silver Acres. Despite his earlier resolve, he had actually enjoyed the ball. And he had enjoyed his dances and the supper he had shared with April. If she were not the adventuress he was certain she must be, he could enjoy having her as a friend. As it was . . .

He began his plan to ingratiate himself with the girl—he had no expectation of impressing Beatrix and considered the brother as merely a necessary third in his plans—the next morning by inviting the three of them to join him in a ride around a section of Silver Acres, saying, "I know you must be interested in seeing everything about the place."

He did not hint that he had been informed by some of the servants, who had no love for the rapacious brother and sister, about their careful scrutiny of every part of the mansion and their evaluation of its contents. Let them do the same about the property, for all the good it would do them in the end.

"You may find it worth your while to view the grounds, even if this estate is part of the entail, which means that it goes to the next earl, along with the title," he added in explanation.

"We know what the term means, thank you," Edward Ainsworth said stiffly.

"But I did not know it, of course," April interjected. "Thank you for telling me."

"I know you did not, my dear April, but there is really no reason for you to burden yourself with all of the sordid details about your inheritance," Edward added smoothly. "I am right here to see to all of those matters for you. We should be more interested in seeing April's part of the estate," he said to the other man.

"That would be a more difficult thing for you to do at this time for, aside from a share of my uncle's money, which is in the bank," he had almost said, *where it is safe from you,* but reminded himself in time that he would not convince April of his wish to be her friend if he said such things, "the only unentailed property lies in Sussex, several days' journey from here."

"And of course, you wish that we would go there, leaving you here to continue your efforts to poison the earl's mind against us," Beatrix said in the nasty tone she customarily used when speaking to him.

"It will not be necessary for me to do anything of the kind, Miss Ainsworth," Alan responded. "I am certain that, given enough time, you will be able to do that admirably without any help from me."

He ought not to have spoken to her in that manner, he supposed, cursing himself for letting her make him lose control of his temper again. It would only serve to increase her dislike of him, although he doubted such a thing could be possible. And it might make it more difficult for him to impress April as he had planned to do, although—as he watched her bite her lip to restrain a smile at Miss Ainsworth's flush of anger—he did not think she was so devoted to the older woman that she would take offense at what he had said.

He asked himself why he should take the trouble to be polite to the older lady. Even if Ainsworth and April were who they pretended to be—and he would never own that they were—*she* had no right to be here, except as his uncle's self-invited guest. And as the future Earl of Hannaford, he was finding it wearisome to be treated as if he were some loathsome species of insect.

If looks could be fatal, he told himself, *you would be a dead man this moment, Alan Graves.* Beatrix Ainsworth's face had darkened until it was almost purple, and her green eyes were shooting sparks at him. Determined to ignore her as if he considered her of no importance, he turned once more to Mr. and Mrs. Ainsworth.

"I feel so long a journey as that might not fit into your plans at this time, and therefore you might like to see something of this estate instead, since you will doubtless be here for some days." *Not for many days, however, if I have anything to say about it,* he added silently.

"Could we do so, Edward?" The young woman's voice was eager. "From the little I have had an opportunity to see, it seems so wonderful a place, and I should like to see more."

"You do ride, do you not?" Alan asked. If she owned to knowing even so much as that, it would be a first step in his plan.

The plan was unsuccessful. "I—I do not know whether I can do so or not," she replied. "I have a feeling that I may once have known how to ride, but of course I cannot say for certain." She sighed. This was only another one of the many things she could not remember. *When* would her memory return?

"My dear, I do not think you have ever been on a horse," her husband said, looking slightly uneasy.

Aside from the dread of being forced to mount a horse, there was good reason for him to be uneasy. He was certain that, as soon as they were alone, Bea would haul him sharply over the coals for not having taken her part against Graves, but he had no wish for a brawl with a man so much larger and stronger than he. A man who, in his opinion, was all too prone to turn to violence.

Too, Bea was usually able to fight her own battles, and preferred to do so. Why should he interfere? As unpleasant as the man might be, he would scarcely use force against a woman. It might be wiser, however, if Bea would not continue to goad the fellow—but he could see no way of stopping her from doing so whenever she wished. He had never been able to influence her. She would only see any advice he gave as interference.

"I—I think I must have done." He realized that April was answering his comment. "Perhaps it was in a time before you knew me. When I was still a child. . . ."

Her voice faded. Still, it seemed to her that there had *almost* been a memory, a memory of herself on horseback. She could not see where she was or who else was present, but thought this might be a sign that things would soon come back to her.

Chapter Ten

"Well, even if it has been some time since you have ridden, there should be no problem," Alan assured her. "I can find you a comfortable mount, and the skill will soon come back to you."

"Then I think I should like to do it. Please say that we may do so, Edward."

"It might be too much of a risk, in your present state of health, for you to overtire yourself," Beatrix warned. "You must remember that the doctor said that you must not do anything which was too strenuous."

"But you had me order a riding habit before we came, so you must have thought we would ride sometime while we were here." *Please,* she said to herself, *do not let Beatrix spoil this for me, too.* She did not know why it should matter so greatly, but she knew it was important for her to be able to ride.

There was so little for her to do here, aside from walking about the grounds nearest to the house until she had become quite familiar with them. Edward and Beatrix were kept busy talking with her grandfather or poking about the mansion a great part of the time. They discouraged her from accompanying them or ignored her if she did so, while they discussed the value of various items they saw. For that reason, she had delayed her planned tour of the mansion; she did not wish to follow them about.

She was left alone, with nothing to occupy her time. Aside from that single visit to her grandfather, she seldom had a chance to speak to anyone except Lucy. Now that Mr. Graves was holding out a hand of—she did not think it was friendship, precisely, but at least of thoughtfulness— she hoped she would be allowed to take it.

Edward hesitated, wondering what would be the best way to discourage her, but to April's surprise, Beatrix reversed her earlier opinion and said, "Very well, if that is what you wish to do, April, I suppose there is no reason why we cannot try it. But you must let us know at once if you feel uneasy in any way. You have always been too adventurous for your own good."

"Yes, Beatrix. I shall be most careful." This time the words did not gall so greatly, since Beatrix was agreeing to something *she* wished to do. "When shall we be able to go?" she enquired.

"At any time that pleases you," Mr. Graves told her. "My duties for my uncle are done for the day."

In any case, his duties about the estate were so light that they could easily have been put aside without a question if he had the opportunity of making friends with the girl. Or, he could have asked one of the grooms to take care of matters which could not be postponed. *This*, he felt, was by far the most important task he must face at this time. If there was any delay in completing his customary work, it would be excused if he were able to prove to his uncle that these people were not what they claimed.

"Oh yes, please, let us go at once. That is—as soon as we have changed."

She hurried toward the house, Edward and Beatrix following after her. "Do you think it wise to let her do this?" Edward asked. "If she should fall—"

"I did not think so at first, because I did not wish her to become friendly with that fellow, just as I thought it was not a good idea to permit her to dance with him. But later, I thought better about that, and I have changed my mind about this as well. It might work out for the best, after all. If he chooses her a safe mount, I can see no problem. She will certainly not wish to ride for any distance, if she has not done so since she was a child."

Edward nodded, only half-satisfied, but if Bea said that it would do no harm to allow April to ride, there was little he could do about it. He would have to accompany them, of course, for it would not be proper to permit the girl to go alone. The thought of mounting a horse made him shudder; he definitely did not like the brutes or anything to do with them. April would not know, of course, but he thought that Bea would have remembered that and made some excuse to prevent April from riding.

April scarcely needed Lucy's enthusiastic praise to know that she looked well in her new riding habit. Made of a soft golden brown *velours simule,* almost the same color as her eyes, it was simply cut to mold her figure, and aside from several large buttons of darker brown bone, had been designed without any sort of furbelows.

Certainly it could not compare with Beatrix' striking outfit of brilliant green wool, with its shako and its military trim, but April thought the softer lines of her own habit were vastly more becoming. The other woman could wear so conspicuous an outfit, but she would feel lost in such a costume.

Alan Graves had been true to his word and had found her a gentle, well-mannered gelding whose coat nearly matched the color of her habit. April laughed when she saw it. "We do make quite a pair, do we not?"

"Yes, I could not have chosen better had I known," he said, wondering what she—or what her husband—might say if he remarked that she reminded him of a tiny golden-brown bird, of a kind he did not know. Would such a remark be considered too forward for him to make to a married woman, even if she was pretending to be his cousin? And what had brought such a thought to his mind? He was not given to having poetical thoughts about any lady—especially this one.

April was also wondering—had she only imagined that there had been an appreciative gleam in the gentleman's eyes as he watched her patting her horse and speaking to it as if they were old friends? Or was it only that she had hoped to see it?

She looked guiltily at Edward, wondering if it was not the wrong thing for her to wish for so much appreciation from another man than her husband, but he apparently had noticed nothing amiss. In truth, she thought that he looked almost ill.

"Would you prefer that we postpone our ride until some other time?" she asked him, willing to forgo her pleasure if he was ailing.

Edward shook his head, not daring to answer her, lest his voice betray his uneasiness at the thought of having to go on this outing. Why had he not been able to think of some believable excuse for staying behind today? He might have stumbled on the stairs and pretended that he had sprained his ankle. Beatrix alone would certainly have been quite suitable as a chaperon for April. Still, since he had not been able to think of a reason for remaining behind, it had not seemed the proper thing for him to refuse to accompany them.

Neither his mount nor Bea's seemed to have any marks of distinction. Certainly, they could not compare with the sleek black animal whose reins Graves had looped carelessly over his arm while he caught April around the waist and tossed her to the back of her own horse, then bent to adjust her stirrup. It was most improper for the man to have lifted her in that fashion instead of cupping his hands to catch her foot, but Edward was much too miserable contemplating the ride ahead of them to make any objection, and apparently Bea had not noticed. If she had done, certainly she would have condemned Alan for his forwardness.

"You manage to do yourself rather well in the matter of a horse, do you not?" After several false attempts to speak, Edward was finally able to make the comment in what he hoped would be thought his normal tone.

How—how arrogant *of the man to have so fine an animal to ride,* Edward told himself, unable to repress a faint feeling of resentment at the other's good fortune. It was almost as if he already saw himself as master here. Still, *he* would not have wished to exchange horses with Graves, if he were given the chance to do so. His own mount appeared to be gentle enough—if any horse could be considered gentle—and the black stallion had the look of a dangerous animal.

"Yes," Alan agreed. "Thor has no equal in this part of the country, I am certain. Although he is still a bit young to be racing, he is eager to do so. I have allowed him to run now and then, but only here on the estate where he has no chance to overreach his strength and where I can watch him closely. Uncle made me a present of him the day he was foaled, and I alone have had the training of him. He is a trifle on the spirited side. In fact, none of the grooms would dare to ride him."

"I think he is beautiful," April said, leaning down from her saddle to stroke the black's silken neck. To Alan's great surprise, the stallion appeared to take no exception to the caress, but turned his head to stare up at the person who had dared to touch him, blowing his breath softly in her direction.

"Be careful, April," Edward called. "The beast may bite you."

"I should have thought he would have attempted to do so. Generally, he does not like to be touched by a stranger, and I know I ought to have warned Mrs. Ainsworth not to pat him," Alan said, feeling somewhat guilty at not having done so. It was not a part of his plan to have the girl savaged by his mount, although he owned to himself that he would not have minded in the least had the older woman been so treated. "Except," he added beneath his breath, "I should not like to think of what biting *her* might do to Thor."

"Of course, I should never have thought she would dare to do anything of the kind or I should have prevented her from making the attempt," Alan continued aloud, "but it appears that Thor has found a new friend. Tell me, can you charm all creatures so easily as that, Mrs. Ainsworth?"

"I—I cannot say. I have never tried to do so—that is, I do not remember that I have ever done so. It is only that he knows I admire him."

"Well, let him be," Edward ordered rather more shortly than he had intended. He had helped Beatrix to her saddle and now nervously mounted his own horse. The animal, keenly aware of his rider's agitation, danced about for a time before settling down to move along with the others.

The horse's behavior only added to Edward's uneasiness, but he hoped no one would notice his feelings—especially so competent a rider as Graves. It was *not* cowardly, he told himself, to be distrustful of horses, merely because he had been thrown repeatedly as a child. His father, who had been a past master of the local hunt, had brought out his most mettlesome animals and insisted Edward should learn to ride properly. To the old man's great disgust, he had never succeeded in doing so.

Alan was careful not to set too swift a pace, since he could tell immediately that the brother and sister were far from being experienced riders. Ainsworth, it seemed to him, actually appeared to be afraid of his horse. On the other hand, April was leaning forward in her saddle; he suspected that she would have liked to allow her animal to have its head.

"Remember," he said in a low tone so that the others could not hear, "you probably have not ridden for some time. So we must go slowly at first."

"Must we?" she asked, half-disappointed. "It seems such a waste—just to amble on in this way. The horses would like to go faster. Mine especially, and I feel certain yours does the same."

"At first, I said," Alan smiled. "If you have no trouble today and our rides continue, I think you may be allowed to let him out a bit. But I should not wish you to take any chances, as you will find that you are a bit stiff until you have become accustomed to riding once more. Also, I do not think your husband is enjoying our ride as much as you are." He had not intended to call Ainsworth's uneasiness to her attention; still, her husband's attitude toward his mount should not come as a surprise to her.

April had been so happy to discover that she was able to ride that she had forgot that the others were with them. Now she glanced over her shoulder at Edward, noting that he was white faced and trembling. His extreme nervousness was still being felt by his horse, which was beginning to fidget from one side of the path to the other, now and then brushing his rider against some nearby tree.

"No," she said contritely, "it does not not seem that he does. I thought before we left the stables that he did not feel quite the thing, but when I asked if we should wait till another time, he told me nothing was amiss. I think he did not wish for me to miss the opportunity to ride today, since he knew I wished it so much. Still, I suppose you are right and we should not stay out too long, this time. But can we go again?"

"As often as you like—if there are no objections to our doing so." It was entirely possible that Ainsworth would not permit her to ride with him again. If riding overset him as greatly as it appeared to do, he might well feel that it was not the thing for his wife to attempt.

Alan hoped he was wrong about being able to obtain Ainsworth's permission for further outings; the girl had not looked so happy at any time since they had come here as she did now. It seemed that it took so little to please her—or was that merely a part of her act? Once more, he felt confusion about her actual role in the scheme to cheat him.

Content with Alan's promise, April soon turned her horse toward the stable yard. "Oh, that was wonderful," she cried as she slipped from the saddle to the ground. "And Mr. Graves says that we may ride as often as we like. Will you not enjoy that?" she asked of the others.

"I do not think—" Edward began, fearing that he might be forced to ride out again. Was there no way he could avoid a repetition of today? He would break his leg if necessary, to do so.

Before he could complete his objection, Beatrix said, "I see no reason why you should not go out whenever you wish to do so. However, like Edward, I do not think that it will be necessary for both of us to accompany you every time you ride, and there are times when we shall have other things to occupy us."

"But—" Edward began, but she gave him no time to say more.

"If you enjoy riding, as you certainly seem to do," Beatrix continued, "and if Mr. Graves has no objection to having your company from time to time, it might be that the exercise would be good for you, April."

Far from objecting to this arrangement, Alan could think of nothing that would please him more. He could have hoped for no better way of getting the girl's confidence than to encourage her to continue a sport she enjoyed, but knew that he could get no information from April as long as the other two were present.

Once the two of them were alone, however, he was certain he could soon manage to persuade her to give him some of the details he desired. Too, she seemed so happy when they were riding that it would truly be shameful to deprive her of the sport. If he could provide some enjoyment for her at the same time he was achieving his own purpose, what was wrong with that?

"I should be happy to take Mrs. Ainsworth about whenever she wishes," Alan said. "There are a number of excellent rides on the estate."

Edward frowned, unable to believe that any ride could be enjoyable, but Beatrix nudged him sharply with her crop until he said, "Well, I cannot see that there would be anything wrong with your riding without me, as you will not be going off the estate. Only you must be careful not to allow April to overtire herself. Remember that she still is not entirely well."

"Oh, Edward, you know that the doctor said I was well, except for my lack of memory," April protested. "And that it would be a good thing for me to exercise."

"But not strenuously," Edward reminded her.

"There is nothing strenuous about riding—not with so wonderful a horse as this one. All I need do is sit still and allow it to do all the work. I feel so much better, even after so short a ride. I *know* now that I have ridden in the past, and I am certain it will be good for me. As long as Mr. Graves does not object to guiding me about, of course," she added, wondering how long his good will might last. She recalled how quickly he could change from considerate to sarcastic about her role here, just as he had done at the dance.

"Yes," Edward agreed, "but you must remember he also said that you must not do too much. So if I agree to allow you to ride, you must promise to be careful."

To Edward's surprise, Beatrix said, "I am certain April will take care. And Mr. Graves has promised to see that she does not overtire herself."

Since his sister had said that, Edward saw no choice but to nod his approval of the girl's going.

As he and Beatrix walked toward the house, he glanced back to April who was standing by her horse's head, stroking its nose and speaking to it in soft tones, while Graves stood watching her, the reins of his own mount looped over his arm.

"What was the reason for all that?" he demanded of Beatrix.

"Why not let her go when she wishes—and without us? You know that you do not enjoy riding." She did not mention the fact that riding clearly terrified him; it would be best to spare him the humiliation of knowing his fear was so obvious to others. "And it is plain to be seen that April does so."

"She might be thrown," Edward said. "It could be dangerous for her. Who knows—"

"I do not think we need worry about that," Beatrix interrupted. "Mr. Graves appears to have chosen her a good horse. And she promises to be careful."

"That may be, but you must realize that Graves will be making the most of this opportunity; doing whatever he can to get her to say something—anything—which he can use to discredit us."

"Certainly that is his object in inviting her—and it seems to me that we might as well give him the opportunity to talk to her, try to pry secrets from her, since that is what he wants." Beatrix continued walking towards the house.

"Then we are playing his game by permitting her to go."

"That is what he will think, but you know he will learn nothing from her—she can tell him nothing. And it keeps him away from the old man just that much longer. The young fool will think he is being clever in his attempts to pry secrets from her, while you and I can laugh at his clumsy efforts. Remember, there is nothing he can find to use against us."

Edward caught her hand and squeezed it. She had thought of a way to foil Graves and, at the same time, to save him from enduring another day like today. "Bea, you are the most wonderful person in the world. I must confess that I had not thought of that reason for allowing her to go with him. And besides, you are right, I do not care to ride."

"And there are so many other things we might do with our time," she said diplomatically.

"You are right again. However, I think April often has a dull time here. This will give her a bit of enjoyment and, as you have said, keep him out of the way while I have an opportunity to entrench our position with the earl."

April had been surprised that Beatrix should urge her to go riding with Mr. Graves. Her sister-in-law had never before agreed to anything she wanted to do.

She was prompt to take advantage of this gift and said to Alan, "You know I should enjoy riding with you whenever you wish to allow me to go, Mr. Graves. However, you should not concern yourself too much about my ability to ride. As I have told Edward, it feels as if I have done it often before. Since Edward says he did not know about my riding, I am certain it must have been in the days before he joined my parents in France."

"And when was that?" Perhaps she would let drop a crumb of information.

He was doomed to disappointment—this time. "I am sorry, but I do not know just when he first came. He says that he was a friend of the family, so he must have visited us from time to time. I hope that I can soon remember. This business of always wondering about myself and my life is so discouraging."

Alan felt a sense of discouragement, as well. So she was not yet ready to talk. Well, it was probably too soon to expect her to give him her trust; this was the first time that he had made any overtures of friendship. He could be afford to be patient—for a time. If she took as much pleasure from riding as she appeared to do, she was certain to forget herself soon and make a statement which would lead him in the right direction.

The next morning as April eagerly dressed to go riding with Mr. Graves, Lucy knelt beside her, fumbling with her boot. "Beg pardon, Madam," Lucy said, "I forgot about this yesterday. I hope you were not put out by not having it."

April looked down to see that Lucy was fastening a spur about the ankle of her boot. She kicked out so suddenly that the maid was overset and fell to the floor, looking up at her in surprise.

"*Not* a spur—I never wear a spur."

Suddenly realizing what she had said, April clapped her hands over her mouth, then reached down to help Lucy to her feet. "I am so sorry for kicking you, Lucy—but you see, I suddenly remembered something. It is the first thing! I am beginning to remember!"

"Oh, Madam, how wonderful for you." The girl furtively rubbed herself, but April noticed.

"Oh, did I hurt you? Please forgive me. In all the excitement of remembering that I hated spurs, I forgot about you."

"Oh, it wasn't nothing," Lucy said, then thought: *Imagine any of the others, especially that old cat Miss Ainsworth, apologizing to a servant for hurting them, meaning to or not.* " 'Tis just so wonderful that you remembered."

"Yes, perhaps this is the start, and I shall soon remember everything. I must tell—"

To her surprise, she realized it was not with either Edward or Beatrix that she wished to share her good news, but with Alan Graves. The fact that she had remembered even one little thing from her past should help to convince him that she was *not* pretending about her loss of memory.

She caught the skirt of her habit firmly, so that it would not trip her as she hurried down the stairs and out to the stables, where he was waiting with the horses already saddled.

"The most wonderful thing has happened," she cried. "I *remembered*!"

Was this to be the revelation for which he had been hoping? Would she tell him what he wanted to know?

"You remembered?" he prompted.

"Oh, not everything, of course. But this morning when Lucy—my maid—was about to fasten a spur to my boot, I remembered that I have never liked to wear a spur. I would not do that to a horse."

Alan looked at her, puzzled. *This* was the momentous news she was bringing him?

April sighed. "You cannot understand, can you, what it means after all this time to remember something. Even so small a thing as that. Perhaps I shall soon be able to remember everything, and can prove that I am truly April Ainsworth."

Hiding his disappointment that she intended to tell him no more, Alan forced a smile. "I suppose that would mean a great deal." He caught her up and lifted her to the saddle. "I had noticed that you did not wear a spur," he told her as he fitted her foot into the stirrup. "But I merely thought it was your custom to ride without one."

"It is—it is. But I did not know it until now."

She sounded almost as if she were telling him the truth. It was a good pretense, he owned to himself. And perhaps, having told him so much, she would soon begin to tell him other things, things which would be more important to his case against the trio.

Meanwhile, he found that he was enjoying her company. His uncle was not given to entertaining his neighbors. He cited his poor health as the reason for not wishing company, which had given his nephew the idea of using that excuse to keep the Ainsworths away from him. Alan suspected, however, that the old man merely preferred to sit in solitude with his memories of his beloved wife.

Because of this dearth of visitors, there was seldom anyone about to accompany the younger man on rides, except for one of the grooms. And when he rode with one of them, he found it annoying to hold his stallion down to a pace the other could match. The few times he had given Thor his head, he had been alone.

To his surprise, he felt no such annoyance when he forced the black to match strides with April's mount. Also, it was pleasant to have another person with whom he could share conversation, even if she did not tell him what he wished to hear.

Chapter Eleven

They were not always alone, however. Virginia and Gilbert Soames, having learned of these rides, soon began to accompany them.

"I have seen you riding about from time to time," Virginia said, making a play with her long lashes, "and should have enjoyed riding with you. But I could scarcely come with you alone—what would Ma*ma* have said—and Gilly has always said he did not care for riding about the countryside."

"A fellow can change his mind, can he not?" Gilbert wanted to know. "Riding is like anything else. It depends upon the company." He brushed his moustache and flashed what he considered a winning smile at April, but she seemed to be unaware that he had just complimented her.

Alan could scarcely say that they were interfering with his plans or that he wished to be alone with April. The others would have leaped to the wrong conclusion. Nor could he confide that he hoped to persuade the young lady to own that she and her companions were planning to cheat him. He welcomed his neighbors' company with the best grace he could manage.

It seemed to April that Virginia chattered endlessly. She

spoke of the many affairs she had attended during her Season in London, of the crowds of admirers who had followed her about. More than once she mentioned having encountered someone she called "Prinny," who, according to her, had been most attentive to her at some ball or other. April had no idea to whom she was referring, but it was not surprising to her that any gentleman would be attracted to someone as lovely as Miss Soames.

Only two such rides were enough to dull Virginia's enthusiasm. Of what use was it to speak of her triumphs to someone so green that she could not comprehend what it meant for a young lady in her first Season to have attracted the attention of the Prince Regent, even for a moment? Too, Alan Graves did not appear to understand her hints that he should allow April to ride with Gilly while he spent some time with her.

"I fear we cannot ride with you tomorrow," she said at the end of the second ride. "I must go to Bedford, and Gilly must accompany me."

"But—" Gilbert began.

Virginia did not allow the protest. "You know I cannot go alone." Not that she would have found it necessary to do so. A footman, coachman and her abigail would be adequate chaperonage, of course, but that did not matter to her. She knew what was in Gilly's mind, but if he would not help her in her quest, she did not intend to help him.

Alan expressed insincere regret, and April murmured a few words. She was not unhappy that they would have no other company. Now that Alan was no longer being censorious, she much preferred to ride alone with him.

There was no longer any thought in Alan's mind of openly accusing April of being an imposter. He could not convince himself that she was what she appeared to be, but he found that he was confused as to the true state of affairs.

Sometimes when he was with her, he felt that there was nothing she could tell him—that the moment when she had appeared so excited about remembering a small thing, such as not wanting to wear a spur, meant that she was telling him the truth about her loss of memory. But just as quickly, he would decide that her naiveté was merely a pretense to throw him off his guard.

It took only a short time to learn that April had—whether she had known it or not—been right in her feeling that she had once been an experienced rider, so there was no need for him to watch her carefully to see that she did not overtire herself. In truth, he was forced to restrain her from recklessness. She was forever urging him to race their mounts.

"It would not be a fair race," he told her, laughing, for it seemed this was his chance to win the confidence of the younger female. "You may be riding Mercury, but I assure you he has no wings on his heels."

"Should he have?" She glanced down at the animal's hooves, as if expecting that wings might sprout if she hoped strongly enough.

So she could not remember her mythology—but then, many people would not know such things, so her ignorance in that field meant nothing. Or was this only another effort to deceive him that she had lost her memory? "No, it is simply an expression. What I mean is, that as speedy as he might be, he could never be a match for Thor."

She glanced at the black stallion, then leaned forward in the saddle to stroke the neck of her own mount. "I own that your Thor appears to be capable of great speed. Still, I should like to try to race, for I have more faith in Mercury than you do. Perhaps the two of us might manage to prove you wrong."

"No chance of that, I can assure you. But if you wish a gallop, I do not see why we should not do so. When we reach the meadow, of course, where there are no hidden obstacles. Not before," he warned.

"Yes, I should enjoy that very much. And I can wait until you say it is safe—although I should like to begin this moment."

As she promised, she rode sedately until he nodded to show they had reached the spot he meant, then urged her mount forward. Thor was eager to do the same, so Alan loosed his tight rein, giving him the signal to go ahead. Young as he was, the stallion had to be discouraged from straining his muscles, but he acted as if he had raced from the day he was foaled. *He is quite as reckless,* Alan mused, *as the girl.*

Side by side, the two horses galloped over the smooth field. Difficult as it was, because the animal did not like any sign of competition, Alan held Thor back so that he and April reached the far side of the field at the same time.

"Oh, that was wonderful," she cried, pushing her hair back from her brow. He could see the faint mark of a bruise on her temple. Either she had truly been injured at some time, or the mark had been carefully applied to add verisimilitude to their tale of an accident.

For an instant, he wondered if her husband might have struck her, then shrugged the idea aside. Ainsworth did not appear to him to be the sort who would behave violently, even to a young girl. Alan told himself he would not say the same about the sister. In his opinion, nothing would be beyond that one. A regular cockatrice, in his opinion. The girl's life must be miserable with that witch breathing fire at her.

Judas, he thought, as he watched her walk ahead of him to the house, *am I beginning to feel sorry for her?*

He warned himself he must not be taken in by April's air of innocence, that all of this was merely a part of the plot to steal a share of his rightful inheritance. After all, he was not some green lad, to permit himself to be hoaxed by a pretty face.

Having so warned himself, he then turned cat-in-pan and decided that she might be only a pawn in the schemes of the other two. In all his life he had never been so uncertain of anything as he was when he tried to decide whether or not she was what he now owned to himself that he wanted her to be—innocent of any thought of wrongdoing.

"Is she a cheat, or has she been tricked into taking a part in this scheme?" he said aloud, but the only one who heard him was Thor, so he received no answer. Even if he had one, Alan told himself with a laugh, what good would it have done? Thor *liked* her. And did he? Another question he could not answer.

Whichever opinion of her was the right one, however, he was positive she must know *something* of what was in the minds of the other plotters, and it would be wise of him to be most careful when he was with her, lest, in his attempts to learn something from her, he might instead present her with the sort of information with which she and her friends were seeking to discredit him. In this way, his thoughts went backward and forward, first blaming, then exonerating her, until he thought it was fortunate that no one should ask his feelings, for he could not have told.

Merely because he did not trust her—or did he?—did not mean that was a reason for them to curtail their rides together. He was finding them as enjoyable as she appeared to do. It seemed, too, that neither Ainsworth nor his sister gave a thought to what April did, as long as she was not underfoot.

Nor, he decided, did either of them appear to have the slightest worry that he might learn the truth from her while they were alone. They must have known he would attempt to do so; still, they allowed her to be in his company as much as she liked. Either she had been drilled by the fellow and his she-wolf of a sister until she was letter-perfect in her role of the girl who had lost her memory in an accident, or she truly did not know that she was merely being used by her companions to pretend that she was an heiress. Or rather, that she would be an heiress one day, should they be able to convince his uncle to claim her as his grand-daughter.

Alan owned that he was becoming more bewildered with every day that passed by April's role in all of this. Was she an adventuress, or merely a pawn? Each day when they rode, he questioned her as to whether she had remembered anything else, but she always shook her head and told him sadly that nothing else had come to her.

Was she telling him the truth, or was that a part of the character she was playing? Still, whichever role was the right one, he continued to hope that she would soon tell him *something* which he could carry to his uncle to prove their trickery.

"There is one thing of which I am completely convinced," he told himself. "That other pair are naught but a brace of frauds—even if she turns out to be only their tool. And I shall expose them before I have done with this farce."

Meanwhile, these rides were a pleasant change from what he now realized had been the monotony of his days at Silver Acres. Her naivete, whether it was real or assumed, was something which was refreshingly new to him.

He had spent several seasons in London, but during the last one, when the word had gone around the ton that he was now the heir of the wealthy Earl of Hannaford, the young females had thrown their handkerchiefs at him so relentlessly that he had been happy to escape to the quiet of the country.

Not, he reflected, that he could say he had been shunned by them when he was no more than a captain. Far from it. He had blamed their pursuit at that time on the attraction of his regimentals, but knew it was he, not the scarlet coat, that drew them. The promise of a title and its accompanying fortune for the female who captured him had only made the chase more frantic.

It was not until now that he recognized that he had actually been hungering for company, especially the company of an attractive female, since he had come here. Now he had that company; a pretty girl who seemed to be enjoying these rides as much as he. *Female* company, he reminded himself, forced to hide his irritation on the occasions—far too many of them for his peace of mind—when Gilbert Soames appeared just as they were about to ride out. Virginia no longer came with her brother, but Alan told himself that she was certainly not missed. Virgie was naught but a chatterbox, full of her own importance—nothing like the quiet company April offered.

Oddly enough, April did not appear to care in the least that he was determined to prevent her from getting any part of his uncle's estate. It must be nothing more than a pretense on her part, of course, or so he tried to convince himself. But whatever it might be, these outings were, at the least, a pleasant change from the continual round of invitations he had received in London. Yes, that was why Virgie irritated him; her talk was too reminiscent of those days.

Sometimes they visited the tenant farms, where he would present April merely as Mrs. Ainsworth, who was a visitor to the estates. On one occasion he took her to the cottage of Nanny Goodall, who had been Arthur's nurse. If she were ever to give herself away, he thought, this would be the time. It would be impossible to keep up the pretense before those old, but quite sharp eyes.

It was he who was surprised by the result of the visit. The old lady peered closely at April, then caught both her hands. "You are!" she exclaimed. "I know it. You are my boy's little girl come home. You may not remember me, my dear—"

"I am sorry—" April intended to explain her loss of memory, but had no opportunity to do so.

"No—you could not remember. You were little more than a babe when your father brought you to visit me. It was so long ago—then we thought you were lost along with him and his good wife. Heaven be praised that you were spared to us."

Tears were streaming down her face, and April blinked back her own tears as she bent and kissed the wrinkled cheek. "I am so happy to be here," she said softly. This old woman, at least, did not doubt her. Now she knew this was where she belonged.

Alan felt his throat tighten as he watched the two of them. If Arthur's old nurse recognized April, was that not a sign in her favor? Or did the old woman truly recognize her? Was it possible for her to do so, when she had last seen his cousin as a small child?

Hannaford had said she had changed so much since she was here last that he would not have known her, so how could Nanny Goodall do so? Perhaps it was only that the nurse had heard what was being rumored by the other tenants, and had convinced herself that the earl's granddaughter had been returned to the family.

Despite his care in not saying anything of the kind, he knew that the house servants would have spread the word about her reason for being at Silver Acres. He doubted there was a tenant anywhere on the estate who did not already know that the young woman was claiming—or at least, her husband was making the claim for her—to be Hannaford's granddaughter. Since she did not put on the "lady of the manor" airs so hopefully adopted by some of his female friends, but greeted each of them as if she hoped they would be friendly, she had soon made many friends throughout the estate.

When one of the farmers addressed her as "my lady," she smilingly returned his greeting, then turned to Alan with a puzzled look and said, "It is not right that he should call me that, is it? I like the sound of it, of course, but I do not know—"

"No—the man was merely being polite when he address-ed you in such a manner. There could never have been a Lady April, unless Arthur had succeeded to his father's title." This was the law, of course—but by speaking as he did, he avoided saying again that he did not consider her to be his cousin's daughter.

He knew, of course, that all the tenants, even Nanny Goodall—who would be heartbroken to learn she had been mistaken—would slam their doors in her face instantly if it turned out that she was an imposter, for they had a fierce loyalty to the estate. For the time being, however, everyone accepted her right to be here, just as the old nurse had done. No word from him could have convinced them otherwise; she would have to do that herself, unless his uncle received word from France of their fraud.

He still had not been able to get his hands on those all-important papers, but did not give up hope of finding where his uncle had put them. Without them, the trio might as well leave Silver Acres, for they would no longer have a chance to make good their claim. He would not miss the company of the others, especially the viper-tongued Beatrix, but owned to himself that the place *would* be less interesting when April was gone.

There were days when the weather did not permit them to ride, although April was so eager for the sport that she had to be restrained from going out with no regard for rain or fog. Only the threat that the earl might forbid her riding entirely, if she was too reckless, held her back.

On these days, Alan guided her about the interior of the mansion, showing her many of the treasures that were his favorites. Here at least, they were free of the company of Gilbert Soames. Gilly was not interested in treasures, except the sort which could be spent at the gaming tables.

Alan was careful to choose times when Ainsworth was occupied in some other part of the building, telling himself that his reason for eschewing other companions was that he was still hopeful April would tell him what he wished to hear—certainly not because he preferred to have her company to himself, without Ainsworth's watchfulness or his sister's biting remarks.

April was the perfect companion for such a tour of this place he loved, because this was what she had wanted to do. If she were truly Arthur's daughter and had traveled with her parents, she must have seen a number of fine palaces, but she viewed everything about this place as if it was something she had never known. Was this yet another sign she was an imposter, or that she truly could not remember?

She gazed in wonderment at the enormous chandeliers with their myriads of crystal drops, at the ceilings painted with allegorical figures, at the numerous pieces of marble statuary—many of which, he told her, had been brought from Italy at one time or another—and at the ornate furnishings filling room after room. For generations, the family had collected the best, and sometimes the worst of the treasures of the world, and every room was filled with their booty.

"At least," he told her, "uncle has not given in to the popular movement in London—that of using crocodiles or sphinxes as part of the furniture."

April merely stared at him, her brow wrinkled as she appeared to be trying to understand him. "Crocodiles," she repeated. "Sphinxes? What are they?"

He decided to humor her this time; pretending he thought

she truly did not know such things might be the best way of winning her trust. "Crocodiles are scaly animals with long tails, short legs, and very sharp teeth, while the sphinx is supposed to be a creature with a human head, but the body of a lion and the wings of a bird."

"But who would want such things as that in the house?" Her bewilderment sounded genuine.

"Oh, they are merely imitations of the real things, of course, done in wood and plaster," Alan replied. "But there has been quite an interest in all sorts of Egyptian objects since the battle of the Nile."

April wondered what battle that might have been, but decided that she had already asked too many questions about such things at the present time, so merely nodded as if his explanation had made everything clear. At some other date, she would try to find out more of what he meant. All these bits might mean something to her when she could put them together.

"Did you not notice," Alan asked, "while you were in London, how many hostesses now have table legs in the form of crocodiles?"

"I—I cannot recall having paid any calls, although we must have done when we were there. But that would have been before my accident, so I cannot say—"

So that was the way she intended to act, still saying she had no memory. He found he could only shrug, and said, "Believe me, it is not an attractive fashion, and we can only hope it will not live long."

When they reached the bedchamber of the late countess, however, she needed no explanation of its use. Instead, she moved softly about the room, touching each bottle and jar with gentle fingers, as if she expected the owner to appear and share her joy in them.

"Everything here and in the adjoining rooms," Alan told her, "has been kept exactly as it was while my aunt was alive, even to having fresh flowers placed upon her desk each morning."

April exclaimed with delight at the thoughtfulness of keeping up these rooms. It seemed a fitting tribute to the painted face which smiled down upon them from above the mantelpiece.

"That is a wonderful thing to do for her," she said softly, gazing at the lovely lady's portrait. Would anyone ever think so much of her? She doubted that Edward would do so—at least, not if Beatrix could prevent it.

Alan nodded. "Yes—my uncle adored her, and was brokenhearted at losing her. So much so that he has become something of a recluse. I was not here then, but have been told about it. He gave orders soon after her death that the servants were to treat the rooms as they had done while she was alive."

She silently agreed. Such an action would have seemed impossible from the gruff gentleman of their first meeting, but after her private visit to him, April was not surprised to hear that he might feel this way.

"If the matter were mentioned now, he would doubtless say that he had merely forgot to rescind the order," Alan continued, "which, I can tell you, is far from being the truth; he never forgets anything. He would deny strongly any charge that he is a sentimental man, but I think the care of this room proves how much he loved her."

"Yes, he must have done. She appears to have been a beautiful lady." As he started to lead her from the room, April turned back for another look at the portrait. *I wonder which of the family I might resemble,* she thought. She could see nothing in the face above which was like her own. And she knew that she did not resemble the earl in any way. Perhaps her own mother or father . . .

"She was indeed lovely." Alan leaned against the door frame, gazing up at the portrait, appearing to answer her painted smile. "And she was also one of the most thoughtful people I have ever known. I cannot remember her too well, for I was not here often while your—while my cousin was alive. He was some eleven years older than I, and naturally had little use for a younger lad following him about. But when I did come here, Aunt Laura was very kind to me. My own mother had died when I was six years old, so Aunt tried to take her place as much as she could."

Why am I telling her all this? he wondered. It could not matter to her.

Chapter Twelve

It had mattered, however, far more than he could have realized. April put her hand on his arm, withdrawing it instantly after he had glanced down at it. When Alan acted as he had been doing these past days, she found that merely being with him made her completely happy. So much so that she feared she might reveal just how much she enjoyed his company.

Lest he suspect how warm her feelings toward him had grown, she said quickly, "At least, you can remember what your mother was like, if only dimly. I have been told that I had my mother until sometime last year, but now I cannot remember anything about her."

Her own loss was brought vividly to mind by her words, and she walked across the room quickly to stand with her back toward him, fingering the dainty window curtains, so that he would not see her tears.

Alan felt a brief surge of pity for her, but fought it down, telling himself that he must remember that this was merely a part of the role for which she had been trained. Or could it be the truth? She was no child of the streets, he was certain. Either she had once been a part of a family which loved her or had been carefully taught to pretend as much. But what of her grief about not remembering her parents? It must be an act, but yet . . .

"You have not seen the rest of the family portraits. They are in the Long Gallery," he said, surprised at the gruffness in his tone.

April blinked several times in an effort to hide the signs of her weeping, brushed at several tears which had escaped, then forced herself to smile as she turned toward him. "That is right. You promised that you would show me all the Hannaford ancestors."

"Not all of them are Hannafords." He noted that she had not said, "all our ancestors." Was that merely her way of speaking, or might it mean that she had certain qualms about claiming them as relatives?

"Not Hannafords? Then who are they?" April asked, surprised.

"The family name, you must remember, is Graves. It is my uncle's name, as well as my own, since my father was his younger brother. It was only those few gentlemen who were ennobled—earls, as well as the viscounts who had the title before the earldom was awarded, who were permitted to call themselves Hannaford. And their wives, of course, could use the title."

"Of course," she agreed. This was something else she must have known at one time, she supposed. Certainly her father, who one day would have come into the title if he had lived, would have taught her something about his family's history. His name must have been Graves, also—and hers, before her marriage.

She recalled that when they first arrived, Edward had said her father had been a viscount, but did not think his title had been Hannaford. Why had it been different—and what had it been?

And what of her mother's people, she wondered. No one, not Edward or even the earl, had told her anything about them. Perhaps they had thought it would be better for her if her memory was allowed to return without their prompting, but she wished that they—or someone—would tell her more about her family.

She would have to try to find them when her memory returned. They must be anxious to see how she had grown— unless there had been a quarrel between the families over her mother's marriage. Could that be the reason behind the silence about them?

She stifled a sigh as she followed Alan away from the countess' rooms toward the Gallery. *When* would she know the answers to all of these questions?

The Long Gallery was rightly named, stretching almost the entire north side of this floor. "Why did they choose the north side?" she asked, thinking that another location would have been less gloomy.

"So that none of the portraits would be struck by the direct rays of the sun," Alan replied. "It is supposed to be fatal to the life of paintings. Or so I have heard; I confess that I truly know little of art. Unlike many people, from our Regent down."

"I see." This information about light harming the portraits was something else that she must have heard some time, she supposed, along with so many other matters which seemed strange to her but which everyone else appeared to take for granted. What a number of new things—new to her, at least—she was hearing today. About crocodiles used in furniture and about light harming portraits. Perhaps if she asked enough questions about such matters, one of the answers might start her memory to working once more.

Even while she told herself that she should learn what she could, she forbore to ask about the Regent who was supposed to be so knowledgeable about art. Alan seemed so certain she would know, just as he expected her to know so many other things and, if she had asked anything more, would doubtless have thought her as witless—as witless as she truly was.

At some time in the past, the portraits must have been more widely spaced along the walls, but had been crowded together as more and more were added to the collection. She could see several places where the paper was not as faded as in others, showing that it had been covered for some time.

Only a few such bare places remained, however. It would be a difficult matter to find room for many more portraits along this wall.

"What do you think they will do when they have to put up others?" she asked, thinking that some of the older ones were so dim now, despite having been protected from the sunlight, that they could scarcely be recognized.

"Doubtless they will store some of them in the attics." Alan's tone was light, as if all these ancient ancestors were not of great interest to him. In truth, he was extremely proud of his line, but had become accustomed to hiding his feelings when some of his fellow-officers had accused him of being over-boastful about his connections. "I think it might have been as well if they had done so with some of these."

"Yes—but, of course, they would wish for everyone to see how far back the line reaches," April said.

Alan nodded. "The tale is that there was one, at least, who came over with the Conqueror. He must have had a great army, for I do not doubt that every old family makes such a claim—but it could be true, I suppose. It is not very like that the name was Graves at that time, as that certainly is not a Norman name. It may once have been something quite different but, as often happens, was distorted when it was translated into English—or he may have earned it as a sort of title because of the great numbers of poor Saxons he sent to their graves."

"How horrible," she said, shuddering. "I should not like to think of such a thing."

"Do not do so, then," he said with a laugh. "After all, most old families must have some horrible tales to tell if one searched for them diligently enough. Those were violent times."

"Not only old times," April said. "Edward has told me something of what had taken place in France before he brought me here. It seems impossible to believe that people should do such things to one another. Can we not find something more pleasant to talk about?"

"Certainly. Now this fat gentleman on horseback is our great grandfather. Or I should have said that he was *my* great grandfather. Your great great grandfather, the third earl."

He had done it again, he berated himself. He had actually spoken as if he believed she was his uncle's granddaughter. What could be wrong with him? Despite his many reminders to himself to beware of becoming involved with her, he could not feel that she was truly the adventuress he had first called her.

April had apparently not noticed his slip of tongue. She was gazing intently at the uniformed figure mounted upon a rearing charger. "How were they able to get a horse to stand like that long enough to be painted?" she wanted to know.

"I doubt if they attempted to do so," Alan replied, grateful that her interest had been more on the portrait than on his words. "I believe chargers were trained to strike out in that way at an enemy—another distasteful subject, I fear—but they could not have stood in that position for long. And especially this one, with so much weight upon its back. It is more probable that the old gentleman merely sat comfortably upon a chair while he was being painted, then the artist painted the horse from memory—or from sketches he had made."

"Oh." She seemed to be disappointed at his answer. "It would be more interesting to think it had been done the other way." Having lost interest in the portrait when she found it was not accurately done, April went farther along the gallery. "Oh, there is the countess—the one who was in the bedchamber. She looks grander here, but I liked the other portrait better. And is that—?"

"The present earl. Painted long ago, of course, while his wife was living."

"He was quite a nice looking young man, was he not?" she said, studying the portrait.

"Not the terror he has become, do you mean?" Alan asked with a grin. "I suppose he may have been, but it seems boastful to say so, for I have sometimes been told that I resemble him."

"Yes, you do." April turned to give his face the same attention she had given the painted one, happy for an excuse to do so openly. His eyes *were* gray, she noted. "Not as he looks now, of course—but when he was younger."

Her praise was slightly embarrassing. Pretending an off-hand tone, Alan continued, "Next to him is—his son." He would *not* make the same error another time, would *not* say, "your father."

However, he heard her whisper the words as she stared up at the young man. It was as if she hoped the portrait would give her some message. At last, she shook her head and turned away.

"No—I cannot remember him. Of course, he would have been much older. But it is all a blank. Is there a picture of—of my mother?"

He had himself under strict control by this time and was able to say, "It was planned, I believe, to have them painted as a couple when they returned to England. They would have been almost the same age as were the earl and countess when these portraits were done. And I suppose their daughter would have been painted at that time, as well. There may be a miniature of the viscountess, but none of the young lady."

April closed her eyes, wishing she could shout at him, "Can you not understand—*I* am that 'young lady.' " But she could not. Since she could not know for certain, except for Edward's word to her, how could she convince this man? Especially when he did not want to believe—when he hoped she would go away and leave him to inherit the earl's fortune?

"All this has been most interesting, but I find that I am rather fatigued by so much walking about," April managed to say. "If you will permit me, I shall go to my room for a time and rest before tea."

Without allowing him time to reply, she turned and walked quickly away. She *must not* weep; not when he could see her. The humiliation of having him see her in tears would be more than she could bear.

She had not realized until now how important it had become to have this gentleman believe in her. After all, if they were cousins, they would certainly meet from time to time—and it would be more pleasant if they could meet as friends.

That was what she said to herself, not willing to own, even in her heart, that what she was beginning to feel about this man was something far different than mere friendship. It was wrong for her, a married woman, even to think of any other man except her husband—and especially of a man who so clearly despised her.

Alan frowned and struck his fist against the wall, narrowly missing the painting of the young viscount. It was a pity that he and April must be enemies. There had been several times today when he had almost—no, when he *had* thought her story to be true. It could not be so, he told himself.

"I shall not permit it to be," he told his cousin's painted image. "I *cannot* believe that she is your daughter." In the months since word had been received of the death of the viscount in France, he had known himself to be Lord Hannaford's heir. The arrival of these people had thrown his plans into turmoil.

He would still become the earl one day and inherit the property which went with the title. Nothing could stop that, not even if he should do something to anger Hannaford. Even if he were exiled from Silver Acres for the balance of his uncle's life—an event he hoped would never occur— it would make no difference to his future. He was the only male heir and, whatever his uncle might decide to do about the girl's claim, the entail could not be broken without *his* permission.

But what if she is telling the truth, what if she is truly Arthur's daughter? something within him demanded, something which could not be denied, however he might wish to do so. Yet he told himself that, regardless of any evidence to the contrary which might be discovered, he would continue to deny it. He must do so.

Silver Acres would be his in time, along with all the other entailed property. Perhaps it appeared that he was being selfish to begrudge the girl whatever lands and money Hannaford might intend to leave her. But there were excellent reasons for his doing so, aside from his doubt of her right to be here—doubt which wavered whenever he was with her, but which returned when he was alone and able to think clearly.

He had made a number of plans for those other estates and for all of the money, as well. There was so much he wished to do to improve the property, to bring some of the estates which had been neglected for several generations up to the nineteenth century manner of living. And he would need a great deal of money if he was to make that many changes.

"It would be a different matter if I could believe that she *is* truly Arthur's daughter. But the entire affair is so contrived," he continued to argue with himself, since he had received no hint of the truth from their observation of the portraits, as he had hoped to do.

She had still claimed the viscount as her father, and had asked to see a portrait of her mother, quite as if she had expected it to be here. That is what an imposter would certainly do. And would the true heiress not do exactly the same? Her attitude proved nothing.

He was determined that he must have that money, no matter what he had to do to make certain of it. He would steal the papers if he could do so, and would use every method in his power to discredit the three of them.

Even April? something within him asked—and he knew that, painful as that would now be to him, he would do just that if it proved necessary. *Nothing* must be allowed to stand in his way.

Irrational as it might be, while he was doing his utmost to dislodge her from the estate, he hoped that his patent—or pretended?—show of disbelief would not be reason enough to cause her to cancel their daily rides together. For the time she remained at Silver Acres, the time until his uncle could be convinced that her papers were fraudulent—if they could be proven to be false or he did not have an opportunity to destroy them—he would enjoy having her company. He knew that, if she were forced to leave—*when* she was forced to leave, he reminded himself—he would miss her far more than he had ever missed another person.

Her enthusiasm about everything she saw, her love of the beauty of the estate, her kindness to the tenant farmers she had met, all these things made her an interesting companion, although he had not yet been able to persuade her to say anything he could use against the trio. *Was there a chance that she* was *actually who she claimed to be?* his mind clamored again. Had he been wasting his time in trying to find such proof of her duplicity?

"No—I am certain the proof must be there," he muttered aloud, "and none of the time I am spending with her is truly a waste, however it turns out."

Having been successful in reaching her bedchamber before giving way to her tears, April dismissed the hovering Lucy and threw herself across the bed, sobbing. Even the maid's sympathy would have been unwelcome at this moment. She had hoped so strongly that seeing the portraits of her parents would bring them back to her memory. There was nothing in the gallery which was of the least help.

The portrait of the viscount had been painted when he was little more than a boy, and could have been any other young gentleman, rather than her father. There was far less resemblance between his portrait and that of Lord Hannaford as a young man than she had seen in Alan's face, so she could not convince herself that he had grown to resemble his father as he grew older. There was nothing there to remind her of the past, and apparently there was no likeness of the viscount's wife—her mother—to be found at Silver Acres. If only she could remember them!

Since the moment when she had remembered that she had never worn a spur, she had hoped more strongly than before for at least another glimmer from her past. Nothing had materialized, and she wondered how she could have remembered even that much. How she had hoped that her rides and talks with Alan Graves would help her to discover something. That hope had been as vain as the others.

There were moments during their study of the portraits that she felt the gentleman was beginning to believe her. Had he not told her the old earl—the one on the prancing horse—had been her great great grandfather? Not long after that, however, he had spoken of her parents as if they were not people she could not have known, and had baldly said there was no portrait of the "young lady."

The present earl, her grandfather, seemed content to accept the papers Edward had brought. Was Alan's refusal to do the same not so much because of a dislike of her—for there were times when she was beginning to feel that he did *not* dislike her—as it was because of his reluctance to face the thought of losing a part of what he had come to consider his true inheritance?

After all, if her parents had not died, all of Silver Acres and other properties would have been hers one day, and she told herself that Alan would then have had nothing. Or would he have become the earl eventually, if he had outlived her father?

April supposed that, since he was a man, he might have done so, and therefore could have claimed the estates as well, but owned to herself that she knew nothing of matters of inheritance. She must have known about such things at one time, but if she had done, they had been erased along with the rest of her memories.

She only knew that she would have been willing to give up all claims to her grandfather's wealth if only she could be certain that she belonged here. If Alan wanted the money so badly, then she wanted him to have it—to have anything in the world he might want.

Not that Edward—or Beatrix—would have permitted her to make a sacrifice of that sort for his benefit, she was certain. Something she was not able to understand was why the prospect of having more money should matter so greatly to them.

From the enormous sums which must have been spent on her new clothing, it appeared that her husband must already be a very wealthy man. Was it natural that one should feel that he—or she, because she was certain Beatrix was responsible for much of Edward's behavior—never had *enough* money to satisfy them?

Alan appeared to be affected in the same way as they, but somehow it seemed that he had a greater right to want the inheritance than did Edward and Beatrix. He was the earl's nephew, while neither of them were related in any way. Edward, of course, was her husband and she knew he wanted it for her, but he and Beatrix would profit by her inheritance, as well.

For some reason she could not—or would not—explain to herself, the refusal of Alan Graves to accept her hurt more deeply than all her disappointment at being unable to recognize her parents. Perhaps it would be the best thing if she did not go riding with him again; if it meant so much for him to have a good opinion of her, it would be more sensible if she were to avoid any future contact with him. For her to be spending time with a man who was beginning to occupy so much of her thoughts made it seem that she was being disloyal to Edward.

For some reason she could not explain, she had not said anything to Edward or Beatrix about her memory of disliking to wear the spur. They should be as happy as she to learn her memory was returning, but she felt that they would prod at her to see if she could recall other things—the sorts of things which would convince the earl of her right to be here. "I must wait until I can tell them more than this, or they will not understand," she said to herself. Alan Graves had not appeared to be impressed by such a small memory, but of course, he did not believe that she was April.

If Edward was aware of the amount of time she and Alan Graves were spending together, he gave no sign. Whenever she saw him, which less and less often these days, he appeared to be quite busy, painstakingly studying the furnishings and art objects in the mansion as if he were attempting to estimate their value. Often, she was certain, he and Beatrix discussed his findings, but he volunteered no information to April, and she did not realize that Alan had purposely taken her into other parts of the estate from those her husband was studying.

She asked Edward once about his preoccupation with these matters, but he had dismissed her curiosity, merely saying, "I am only doing all of this on your account, my dear. You would not be able to do it for yourself. Much of what is in the house is certain to become yours some day, although the property itself must go to young Graves, although it, too, should be yours, as it would have belonged to your father."

"I do not quite understand—"

"The law will give it to the male heir, as little as he deserves to have it. In view of the unfavorable opinion he appears to have of us, I do not think that it would be beyond him to exchange some of these valuable pieces for trumpery objects, should he believe he could do so with no one the wiser."

"Oh, I do not think he would be capable of anything of that kind," she had protested, and wondered as she spoke that Edward did not think it strange she should be so vehement about it.

She did not know why she should defend a man who had more than once described her as an adventuress, but it seemed to her that Edward's accusations were quite as unfair to him as Alan's earlier accusations had been to her. While Alan had been guiding her about the estate, she had come to know that he took great pride in everything he had showed her at Silver Acres. For him to replace any of these treasures with sham pieces for any reason would be unthinkable. At least, so it seemed to her.

Edward only laughed indulgently at her protest and patted her arm. "How naive you are, my dear, but then that is no more than can be expected of you at present, as you have no way of judging the people you meet. The man is a thorough scoundrel. He has proven that time and again since we arrived. Despite your lack of any way to compare him with others, you must realize that much about him as well as I. I feel there is nothing he would not dare."

Chapter Thirteen

"If you have so low an opinion of him, why do you not object to his showing me about the estate?" April would have thought Edward would have wished to keep her as far from Alan as was possible, lest he do her harm. Not that she was worried about the young man's doing anything of the kind. No longer was she certain that he was quite as anxious to have her run off the estate as he had been when they first came. She felt Alan would now like to be her friend. For herself, since he had held her in his arms during the dance, she feared her feelings toward the gentleman were not proper ones for a married lady.

"Oh, I do not mean that I believe you will be in any danger from him," Edward assured her quickly. "Whatever he may be, the fellow would not dare to go so far as that. You must know I should put a stop to your rides at once if I thought he offered any threat to you. No—as far as you personally are concerned, I think Graves merely hopes that he can trick you into telling him something that he can use against us."

"But I cannot tell him anything—" She *had* told him what she had remembered, but it had made no difference. She felt that she should tell Edward about that, but hesitated, and the moment was lost.

"I know that, child. For the present, you cannot. And when your memory does return, what you will be able to tell him will not be anything he wishes to hear. So you may go riding with him as often as you like, with no fear."

"Oh, I do not—"

Once more, he did not permit her to finish her protest. "The exercise is apparently improving your health, and it serves to keep that young fellow away from annoying his uncle with attempts to discredit us. You must admit that is a good thing. If these excursions do not bore you—"

"Oh no, not at all," April put in. "It is all so exciting, and I have enjoyed seeing everything about Silver Acres. It is such a beautiful place. Not that I have seen it all, of course—I believe it would take months to do that much riding about. Also, I have met a number of the tenant farmers." Especially wonderful Nanny Goodall, who had recognized her at once as her father's daughter. She wondered if she should tell Edward about that meeting, but he gave her no time to do that, either.

"That is another good thing. When your grandfather finally accepts you as his heiress, these will be your people while he lives. And doubtless you will learn many things from them which will be of help to us later in keeping a tight rein on Mr. Graves."

His opinion of Alan worried April. She could understand, of course, that Edward was only concerned for her rights, but as the days passed she could also see that Alan Graves had a number of reasons to feel as he did about her. Her father's death had left him the heir to the earldom and, he had thought, heir to all of her grandfather's vast holdings. It was no more than natural that he should resent the arrival of someone who could take a part of that away from him.

"Even if Edward approves of my continuing to ride, I think it would be much the best thing for me," she told herself later in the day, "if I do not spend so much time in Alan's company. When I am at a distance from him, I can think of him as being the complete scoundrel Edward has labeled him—at least, I can manage to do so at times. But whenever we are together . . . "

Despite her determination not to accompany the young man again, she donned her riding habit next morning and walked toward the stables, vaguely wishing that she had something else to wear, that she need not appear in the same garment so often. Of course, Alan had seemed to admire it and, for some reason she did not clearly understand, she was certain he would not like to see her in the elaborate sort of outfit Beatrix wore. Still, it would be nice if she had a new riding habit—something he had not seen before.

Would he be there, she wondered, or would he have had second thoughts about taking her about the estate? Since he refused to believe that she was who she said she was—or at least, who Edward said she was—was it right for her to continue going out with him? Should she not share Edward's distrust and avoid him? But then, Alan had always made no secret about his own distrust of her and, until now, it had not prevented her from enjoying his companionship. Why should today be different?

She knew it was different, however. Different, because she had discovered how very much it meant to her to be with him. A feeling it seemed to her that she ought not to have for anyone except her husband.

As April had been doing, Alan Graves had also been giving a deal of thought to the growing friendship between them. Despite the fact that he certainly did not trust the other two Ainsworths not to do him harm if they could, and felt that he ought to consider that April was tarred with the same brush, there was something about her which appeared to set her apart from her companions. At least, he could no longer convince himself that she was as acquisitive as they.

He told himself that he was becoming far too fond of a young female whom he had every reason to distrust and dislike—one who was, after all, another man's wife. These rides together must cease.

Having made a firm resolution that he would tell her his duties prevented him from accompanying her again, he found himself instead greeting her warmly. How attractive she was in that brown habit, he mused as he waved the groom away and personally saddled Mercury for her, and what a picture she and her mount made together.

Unlike many females he knew, she did not seem to object to being seen in the same habit day after day—or perhaps it was because she realized that it became her better than any other color. She should be painted in that brown habit for her place in the Long Gallery beside her ancestors.

He was doing it again—accepting her as Arthur's daughter! It could not be so, but for a moment, he found that he wished she was not an imposter. How well she would fill the role of lady of the manor. Certain remarks he had heard from some of the tenants told him they thought the same. Had Nanny Goodall truly recognized her, or had she merely hoped the girl was truly the heiress?

As he did?

He reined in his thoughts, at the same time pulling so sharply on Thor's reins that the animal instinctively tried to unseat him, and he was brought abruptly back to the present.

"After yesterday's rain," he remarked to April, hoping his voice sounded more natural to her than it did to him, "some of our usual paths will be much too wet for comfortable riding, and it would certainly be dangerous to attempt to race. But there is a favorite spot of mine which I think you will enjoy seeing."

"I am certain I shall." She would enjoy seeing any place he wished to show her, April knew. It was wrong of her to feel this way about Alan whenever she was with him, but the feeling was beyond her control.

A voice called to them, and they pulled up their mounts as Gilbert Soames rode up to join them. "I feared I would miss you today," he told them. "I was certain you would be planning to ride today, but Virgie kept me waiting more than half an hour while she decided whether or not she wished to go shopping. I told her at last that, if she went, it would be without my company as I had more delightful plans."

"Do not allow us to keep you from them," Alan said a

bit sharply, as if he did not know what drew the young
fop to Silver Acres so often now, when he could hardly be
bothered to come here earlier.

"I am certain you will not do that." Gilbert cast an amo-
rous glance at April, but if she saw it, she gave no sign of
doing so.

Why did he have to come here today? she asked herself.
She had been anticipating this ride with Alan, and it would
not be nearly so enjoyable if this gentleman were with them.
Still, Gilbert was a neighbor and, doubtless, was in the habit
of riding here. She must not give any sign that she did not
welcome his presence.

The uphill path Alan had chosen for today's ride was
not wide enough for the three of them to ride abreast, so
April allowed him to lead the way, wishing that Gilbert did
not ride so closely behind her. They drew rein where the
grove ended just before the hill fell away almost at their
feet. Before them lay the mansion and most of the estate,
surrounded by other far-off estates and farms, reaching to
the far hills.

April drew a deep breath. "How wonderful it is. Thank
you for bringing me here."

Alan dismounted, tethered their mounts to a sapling and
turned to lift April from her saddle. Gilbert, however, had
taken advantage of the moment and reached up to draw her
down, holding her despite her efforts to draw away from
him.

"Thank you for your assistance, sir," she said somewhat
breathlessly.

"Am I not to be rewarded—a kiss, perhaps?" Ignoring
the presence of the other man, he bent toward her until April
could feel his moustache brushing her cheek as she turned
her head away.

"Please—Mr. Soames—"

"Nothing wrong with that," Gilbert pressed closer. "Kiss-
es are exchanged between gentlemen and ladies every day,
and no one thinks the worse of them for that."

He might have said more, but Alan's grasp of his collar
drew Gilbert's intricately tied cravat so tightly about his

throat that he could scarcely breathe. Releasing April, he put up both hands to attempt to free himself.

Alan retained his hold upon the other's collar, shaking him fiercely, then throwing him aside. Scrabbling to his feet and attempting to brush leaves and damp earth from his clothing, Gilbert demanded, "What do you think you are doing, Graves? I am not some village lout to be mauled in this fashion, you must remember."

"Nor is *Mrs.* Ainsworth," he emphasized her title, "some tavern wench to be handled in such a fashion."

"No harm was intended."

"That may be—in your mind—but a gentleman does not force his attentions on a lady without some encouragement from her. And I have seen no such encouragement offered."

"You deserve that I should call you out for this," Gilbert said stiffly.

Alan laughed. "Another word, you young whelp and I shall apply my riding crop to your shoulders. That will make you think again before you so insult a lady."

Gilbert glared at him, but knew the other man would not hesitate to carry out the threat. Careful to remain out of Alan's reach, he untied his horse and rode swiftly away.

Alan turned back to April, who was leaning against the side of her mount. Seeing that she was trembling, he strode to her and drew her gently into his arms. "There is nothing for you to fear," he said soothingly. "He will not return. I made certain of that."

"Oh, he did not harm me, but he frightened me. I have never really liked the man, but I did not dream he would behave in such a fashion." She clung to Alan, feeling that he was the one person in her life on whom she could truly depend.

"In the world in which he moves, such behavior is not considered so wrong, but I knew you would not know about anything of the kind and would not like it. That was why I sent him away."

"I am so happy that you did so."

April's trembling had stopped, but Alan was reluctant to let her go from his embrace. *This* was what he had been wanting, he knew now—to hold her like this, never to let her go from him. One arm still circled her waist, the other hand beneath her chin raised her face toward his, now bending close to her.

"No," she whispered, but despite herself, reached up to meet his kiss.

For a long moment they stood, molded against one another, savoring the sweetness of the caress, as he had known they would do one day. Then April placed both hands against his chest and attempted to push herself away from him.

"No," she said breathlessly. "This is wrong. We must not!"

Alan strove for several moments to draw her back to his embrace, then reluctantly allowed his arms to fall to his sides. There was a feeling of deep loss as she moved away from him. A feeling which was utterly strange to him. He had kissed girls before and had never suffered a pang when the dalliance was ended. There had been many who had clung rather than pushing him away, so that when they did leave, he had watched them go with a sense of relief.

But none of them was April.

"You are right," he agreed. "I ought not to have done that—even though I have been longing to do so for many days. I am no better than Gilbert—worse, in fact, because you trusted me."

"*We* ought not," April's voice trembled. It was taking all her strength not to return to his arms, for she had felt that she belonged there. "For I did nothing to stop you. Rather, I encouraged you. And it was more wrong for me than it was for you. After all, I must not forget that I am a married woman. Edward—"

"Yes, I know." *But he does not care for you in the same way that I do,* Alan wanted to tell her, knowing in that instant it was the truth. For some time, he had attempted to delude himself into thinking that what had stirred him was nothing more than the feeling of attraction any man might have toward such a pretty young girl, but knew now it was an emotion which went far deeper.

And, as she had just said, she was another man's wife. A man who seemed not to have the slightest interest in the young woman he had married. The dream that she might be only someone Ainsworth had hired for the role, that she was not bound, was merely that—a dream. If she were not truly married to the other man, he now knew she would have told him so. He was certain her response to his kiss had been real, not part of an act to fool him, and so was her present regret that it had happened.

Unbidden, there came into his mind the thought that, if only she were free, all of this estate that both of them loved so well might be theirs to share—together. But, as she had reminded him, she was not free.

He walked to the edge of the cliff, stared across the miles without seeing their beauty until he was able to bring himself somewhat under control, then turned back to her. "April—"

She put up a hand to stop him; to stop herself, as well, for more than she had wanted anything—even more than she had once wanted to know who she was—she now wanted the warmth of his embrace once more. "No—we must forget this happened." She knew those were the words she ought to say, but how could she forget the heaven she had felt in those few moments when she had been in his arms?

It was something she had never felt for Edward—April was certain that was true. She could not tell herself, "This was what you must have experienced with Edward before you lost your memory." Had she ever been struck by a feeling so strong as the sense of enchantment she knew with Alan, she was certain that there was no accident which could have destroyed her memory of it. She had never been in love with anyone—until now.

Chapter Fourteen

Of course, she reminded herself, she might have married Edward merely because he had told her she must do so, that it was not right for an unmarried girl to travel from France to England alone with a man. Until that time, she had doubtless thought of him merely as an another family friend, possibly someone she had put into the place of her father, but never someone to love.

Still, Edward *was* the man to whom she was married. That could not be changed by anything which had taken place in the past or by what she had felt in Alan's embrace. "We had best go back," she said dully, the delight she had felt in the loveliness of the countryside fading beneath the pall of her unhappiness.

"Yes." Alan could not trust himself to say more as he clasped his hands to provide a step for her mounting. If he dared to place his hands about her waist to lift her to the saddle, as he had been doing since the first time they rode together, he knew he could not prevent himself from holding her close, kissing her once more, begging her to leave her husband and to go away with him. For love of her, he would even abandon Silver Acres.

He could tell her that, but he knew that she would never permit him to make so great a sacrifice for her. During their rides together, she had time to learn how deeply he loved everything about the estate, and he doubted there was any way that he could persuade her to accept the fact that his love for her was far greater. He must not put her to that test.

Nor could he ask her to face the scandal their flight would cause. A scandal that would tarnish her more darkly than it would him, for in such cases, society always blamed the woman for having allowed herself to be carried away by her emotion. For her sake, he must be strong enough to face the realization that there could be nothing between them.

It was bad enough, he thought cynically, that he had not been able to control his emotions this first time—he who had always prided himself that he would be able to control them under any circumstances. He knew now how wrong he had been to think he could be with her day after day and not give in to his feelings for her. He might tell her—and himself—that it had been Gilbert's behavior toward her that had opened his eyes to the way he truly felt about her, but it was far more than that. Still, he would not place himself in temptation's path another time.

Nor must he tempt her to forget her marriage vows. As little as they appeared to mean to the man she had married, he knew that April would respect them, no matter what she might feel in her heart. What he thought—hoped—she might feel, he told himself, then realized it would be best for her if she did not.

When she was settled in her saddle, he untied the horses and swung atop his own mount to lead the way back down the hill. Neither of them spoke as they returned to the stables, both afraid that a single word would be enough to sweep away their restraint.

Without waiting for help from one of the grooms, April slipped awkwardly from Mercury's back in the stable yard and walked into the house without glancing back at her companion. She held herself stiffly erect, feeling that if she relaxed for a moment, she would break into small pieces.

It was of no help to tell herself that she had not intended to fall in love with Alan Graves; it had happened. Nor was there any way that she could hold him to blame for what had occurred—the man had done nothing at all to make her feel the way she did about him. Nothing except to be himself, much too frequently showing his disapproval of her, and calling her an imposter.

"That is scarcely the sort of behavior which one expects as an encouragement to fall in love," she whispered. "So why is it that I have come to feel that he is the only man in the world for me? And a man I have not the right to care for."

Of course, she had not felt so strongly about him at first, dreading their meetings. But as he attempted to put her at her ease, to teach her something about the estate he loved, her feeling for him had grown every time she saw him. It might have been the shock of Gilbert's advances which had sent her into the comfort of Alan's arms, but she knew she had long wanted to have him hold her, wrong though it was.

For the first time in her short memory, she felt that she was truly an imposter. The fraud, however, did not lie in her claim to be the earl's granddaughter, but in her marriage to Edward. It should never have taken place. He had made it clear to her that he had only married her so that he could bring her out of France safely, but she owed him her loyalty for that. Loyalty that she could no longer give him because her love belonged to another man.

She walked slowly along the hall toward her bedchamber, wondering what she should do. There was no weeping now; this feeling went much too deep to be washed away by tears. The honest thing for her to do, of course, would be to go to Edward without delay, to tell him what had happened—or as much as she could tell without making it seem that Alan was in any way to blame for her change of heart—tell him she had fallen in love with a man of whom he disapproved in every way.

Edward would be quite within his rights to divorce her if he wished, for she knew she was being unfaithful to him in her heart if not in her actions. She was certain, however, that he would not do anything of the kind, for if he should divorce her, he would deprive himself of a share in whatever fortune she might receive from her grandfather—and she knew that the money meant more to him than anything. She might take a lover, or a dozen of them, might behave in such a manner as to bring the censure of the world upon her. She might do whatever she liked and Edward would accept that in order to keep her fortune.

If the earl knew the truth, that she was the sort of person who could love one man while she was married to another, might he not disown her? Then Edward would have no choice but to do the same thing. She would be free. . . .

But if the earl learned what had happened, he might also blame Alan for what had happened. He would then send his nephew away, and she could not—*must not*—be the cause of his doing that. "Silver Acres means so much to Alan now—more, perhaps than I do," she told herself. "Much more than I can allow myself ever to mean to him." Her guilt was something she must keep to herself—along with her love.

Beatrix' door was not completely closed and, as she passed it, she could hear voices from within, Edward's and his sister's, of course. Who else would be in her room at this time? April was surprised only because she had thought they would be somewhere else in the mansion, continuing their inventory of the estate's treasures. But perhaps they were totalling up the value of the pieces they had seen. They would wish privacy for that, lest someone overhear them and tell the earl what they had in mind.

"I do not like all this delay," Beatrix was saying. "It is not good. Not good for us. The matter should have been settled days ago."

"Yes—but I do not see how we can encourage the earl to settle it more quickly. The man has his own methods of doing things and no one can change him. It is doubtful, of course, that he will ever hear from France, so he will have to accept what we have told him."

Would it help in the least, April wondered, if they knew

she had regained a sliver of her memory? It was not enough to prove who she was, but it might encourage them to speak of it to the earl.

"So much the better," that was Beatrix once more, "for who knows what he might hear? Still, as you say, there is little chance he will receive any news from his French associate."

"But waiting for him to realize that he will hear nothing will take time, and I do not know how much longer we can hold off our creditors," Edward said. "It would be fatal to all our plans if they descended upon us here."

April put her fingers to her lips. She had supposed, from the great amount of money which had been spent upon her clothing, that Edward was a wealthy man. Did this worry about creditors mean that he was without funds, that he had been hoping to receive her grandfather's money in time to pay for her all her beautiful things? Also, for the costly carriages and horses with which they had made such a show on their journey here? Were they paupers—or worse, the sort of people who bought expensive things for which they never intended to pay?

What would have happened to them if the earl had refused to see them? What would they have done with all that debt hanging over them—debt which had been incurred due to her hasty flight from her home, for some reason she did not now know?

"Fatal, indeed," Beatrix agreed. "A few demands from them would make us appear to be beggars—or worse. And questions would be asked. The wrong sort of questions. But we have another problem. I believe she may be becoming much too curious."

Who is becoming curious? And curious about what? April asked herself. *Is she speaking about me?* Had she done anything to bring such censure upon herself?

Still, was there anyone else of whom Beatrix disapproved so greatly? Why should it worry Beatrix if April asked about things which had happened before her accident? When had she showed the least curiosity, except in her attempts to learn about her past? She had never enquired into Edward's life before he came to Paris, nor had she tried to learn anything about Beatrix' past. She had sometimes wondered about them, but supposed they would tell her what they wished her to know.

"I am *not* curious," she protested beneath her breath. Then she proved Beatrix right about her curiosity by moving nearer the door so that she could hear what Edward might answer. "It is only because they may say something to help me remember the past," she told herself softly. "I should not do such a thing to Edward otherwise, even if I have heard him say that what he wants here is only my grandfather's money—for himself and Beatrix, as well as for me. I already knew that much. But it is bad enough that I am being unfaithful to him in my heart; I do not wish to become a spy, as well."

"I doubt that there is anything of that kind to worry us." Edward's voice was calmer than Beatrix' had been. "The girl has no idea what we have in mind—and will continue to believe whatever I tell her, I am certain."

"I hope you are right," Beatrix replied.

"I tell you there is no need to worry about *her*. Has she not swallowed everything we said?" Edward continued. "However, I have been thinking that it might be safer if we were to take her away from here for a short time. Graves is not so gullible as she and might hit upon the truth if we are not careful. Perhaps I should suggest we take a visit to the seashore, for the sake of her health—"

"An ideal solution. Then, if she becomes *too* much of a nuisance—"

"No, Bea—I should not want to think of anything of that kind. Not again."

"You were not always so cowardly, if you remember, Edward—or should I say, so considerate, since that is what I suppose you would prefer to call it. There was a time in France, I recall, as you should. You may only have stood by at that time, but I think you raised no objection. So why should you hesitate to do what may be necessary now? There are times when I suspect that you are developing a *tendresse* for *this* whey-faced chit." That was the tone Beatrix used so often in speaking to *her,* but April had never heard her use it to Edward.

Nor had she heard a laugh of the sort he uttered as he said, "That little widgeon? Bea, my dearest Bea, you should know me better than that. Since the first time I saw you, there has never been anyone in my life except you. Have I not given you proof of that more than once? How could I have any feelings for another?"

Scarcely able to credit what she was hearing, April stepped closer, inadvertently brushing against the door. It swung inward and she could see the couple entwined upon the bed.

She gasped and stepped backward as Beatrix raised her head and gave her a triumphant glance over Edward's bare shoulder. As April moved away, she could hear Beatrix say, "We should have been more careful, but I thought she was safely out of the way for several more hours. However, that settles the matter for us, I should think. Now you have no choice—or I suppose I must—after all, I know *I* can do what must be done. I am not so squeamish, as you have reason to know."

April turned and fled toward the stairs, hardly knowing where she was going. All she knew was that she must get as far away as possible. How could she have been with the two of them as long as this without suspecting . . .

The long skirt of her riding habit slipped from her nerveless fingers and tangled beneath her feet. As she felt herself falling head first, she reached out, hoping to catch the stair rail, but her fingers merely brushed it painfully while she tumbled over and over to the foot of the long staircase.

Alan had left her to go ahead, hoping that he could reach his own room without encountering her. Only by staying far from her could he keep his intention not to touch her again. After having threatened young Soames for making advances to April, he had behaved quite as badly. No, his actions had been worse. The fact that he had come to love the girl was no excuse for what had happened.

He had resolved that he would tell his uncle that he had received a message from a friend who urgently requested him to come to London. There was no fear that Hannaford would object to his going away for a time; his absence would mean that there would be less trouble about the estate while the old man completed his verification of April's papers.

Once he had reached London, he could invent any number of excuses for not returning to Silver Acres while April—and her husband—were in residence. As soon as she was acknowledged as the earl's granddaughter, the trio would wish to travel, to inspect the estates which would then belong to her. Should they come to London for the season, he could travel elsewhere. The world was wide—wide enough that he need not meet her again, even if he could not forget her.

He was approaching the front door when he heard April shriek, then the sound of her body striking step after step until she had reached the foot of the stairs. Thrusting aside the footmen who had also heard her and had been drawn by curiosity into the hallway, he hurried to the spot where the girl lay in a heap.

"You should not move her until we can call a doctor, Mr. Graves," Wilcox warned him, but Alan ignored the old man and gathered April into his arms, noting with relief that, while she appeared to be somewhat stunned by her fall, it had not been fatal.

"April, my darling girl, how did this happen?" he asked, helping her into a more comfortable position against his shoulder. "I knew I should never have let you go. Did you tell him, and did he strike you, knocking you down the stairs? If he did this, I swear I shall kill him. April, please speak to me."

The girl shook her head, put both hands to hold it steady, and winced at every movement, as she looked up at him.

"Why do you call me April?" she wanted to know. "My name is Caroline—Caroline Kingston."

Chapter Fifteen

Alan's fingers tightened on her shoulders and he shook her until her head bobbled back and forth and her teeth chattered. The concern he had felt for her well-being was completely overcome by a sudden flareup of anger.

"So I was in the right about you, all this time," he shouted, nearly tempted to throttle her for having deceived him, forgetting for the moment that this was the girl he had just told himself he would love forever. "You have no right to be at Silver Acres—to be trying to victimize my uncle. You are not April Ainsworth!"

"Of course I am not." She struggled, pressing her hands against his chest in an attempt to free herself from his furious grasp, but was unable to do so. "Why should anyone think that I am? As I said, my name is Caroline Kingston."

"You knew—you were certain that you would soon be unmasked," he raged, "that you could not keep up the pretense of a loss of memory any longer, so now you are willing to own to the truth of why you came here."

Suddenly realizing the incongruity of his position, seated on the lowest step of the staircase, holding the girl in his arms, yet accusing her of having attempted to defraud him

161

of his inheritance, he grinned ruefully. The realization however, did nothing to dampen his anger.

"No—no, that is not it," she was protesting. "It is nothing
of that kind. This entire affair is all . . . all wrong, somehow. I do not know why it has happened the way that it
did, but I can remember everything now. Not just a tiny
bit, as happened before. I know all that we have been doing
these last weeks, as well as everything which happened in
my life before the accident. Perhaps I struck my head when
I fell downstairs and it has jolted my memory. The fall—
or the shock I had received—may have had something to
do with it."

She shuddered at the recollection of the scene she had
witnessed upstairs, but knew at once that it meant she was
released from a marriage that had never existed. She was
free—free of Edward. But not yet free of her present entanglement. Somehow, she must make Alan understand what
had taken place—although she could scarcely understand it
herself.

"I had left my most recent employment and was on my
way to London in an attempt to find a new position. I was
a roof passenger, since it was necessary for me to save as
much money as I could do, in case I could not find work at
once, as could have happened since my last employer had
refused to give me a character. The horses ran away; I think
the young gentleman who took the lines was unable to hold
them. There was an accident of some kind, perhaps he tried
to turn the team at that speed, and the coach overturned.
I remember how terrified I was when I felt myself falling
with no way of holding onto the coach top. The next thing
I knew, a doctor was asking me who I was—but I did not
know."

"Quite a romance, I must say. And am I now expected
to believe this, rather than the tale you and your friends
have been spinning since you came here?"

His anger was quite as much at himself for having been
fooled by her, as it was at her for hoaxing him. He wished
that he could believe her now, but the change of story came
far too conveniently to be convincing. Was this merely her

way of informing him that she was free, that she was not Edward Ainsworth's wife?

As fond as he was of the girl—as much as he knew he loved her, he corrected himself—nothing could change the fact that she was now admitting that she had come here with her companions in an attempt to take away a great part of his inheritance. Was he expected to overlook her involvement in the plot merely because he had yielded to the temptation to kiss her?

"I do not care whether you believe me or not," Caroline said crossly, drawing herself out of his embrace, wondering what had gone wrong now, what had happened to the man who had so recently held her against his heart and won her own heart with his caresses. The man who blamed her now and had labeled her an adventuress, was not the Alan she had known and had grown to love these past days.

"I *am* Caroline Kingston, a governess," she said with as much dignity as was possible for one in her position. "Or at least, I had been a governess until recently. And I cannot understand why Edward and Beatrix should have told everyone that I am April Ainsworth."

"It seems a fantasy—but I believe you are telling the truth this time." Alan could see, in a way, that such a thing might happen. If only she was being truthful with him now, he told himself, if this meant that she had never been Ainsworth's wife, had not been an adventuress chosen for the role . . .

Caroline could hear the change in his voice, a new note that thrilled her because she could sense that he understood what she had undergone. The hands holding her shoulders were gentler now, caressing rather than punishing.

Confused as well as pleased by his sudden change from deep suspicion to belief, she replied sharply, "Of course I am telling the truth. Why should I lie about it? I have never had anything to hide. Somehow—I do not know how it happened—Beatrix and Edward found me in Dr. Ward's surgery. Beatrix came first, I recall, then she went away and Edward came. They said they recognized me—but they must know I cannot be April. Did Edward not say he had married me in France?"

"That is what he told my uncle."

"But that is all wrong. I have never been in France, so he cannot have met *me* there, as he said, and could never have mistaken me for April if he ever knew her. He never saw me until the day he came to the surgery. But it was not true that Beatrix has not been in France. She was there—and with him. I heard her say so. Edward's talk of a marriage because he and I—he and the real April, I should say—could not travel back to England alone, that was—was not—" The words reminded her once more of the scene which had sent her fleeing from the floor above. "And Edward and Beatrix are not brother and sister, at all— they are *lovers*!"

"Then you are not married—not Mrs. Ainsworth?"

The happiness in his voice was echoed in her answer. "Not Mrs. Ainsworth, nor Mrs. anyone."

"That is wonderful!" Unmindful of the gaping footmen and of Wilcox' disapproving stare, he drew her close once more and kissed her soundly.

"No." She tried to draw away. "You must not." Then she yielded to the strength of his arms, the heaven she had felt in his kiss. *This* was the man she knew she loved; the one who had questioned her so angrily had gone and she hoped he would never return to taunt her again. The paradise she had found when he had held her in his arms on the hilltop was there as it had been, but . . . "But you ought not. I am not—"

"You are not married—that is all that matters to me," Alan interrupted.

"But you forget—I have been an imposter," she said.

"But an unwitting one. I have thought so for some time and know it now. We must tell this to my uncle. He will wish to know—"

"Sir!" Edward was standing at the top of the stair, glowering down upon them. He had overheard enough of their conversation to realize that the girl could no longer be deceived into thinking she was April Ainsworth. She had just declared she could not be his wife, as they had claimed her to be. Her memory must have returned as suddenly as the doctor had said it might do. This could mean the ruin of all their schemes.

Still, if there was some way—if he could manage to play the part of the betrayed husband convincingly enough, he should be able to convince everyone else, especially Lord Hannaford. His belief was all-important to the success of their plans. It did not matter what the younger man might say or do. His entanglement with the girl could be used to their advantage.

"That is my wife you are embracing, sir. You will have the decency to unhand her immediately, although it is wrong to speak of decency to one who is behaving as you are doing. Are you planning to ravish her here, in the sight of all these servants?" Edward spoke angrily, descending several steps, as if he meant to separate them by force. "Am I expected to understand, April, that this is the sort of thing which has been going on when I permitted you to ride with him? Do your vows mean nothing?"

Alan rose to face him, drawing Caroline to her feet and holding her close against him, feeling her shudder as she looked at Edward. What had she seen above stairs to give her this sudden revulsion for the fellow?

There was something more than the fact that she now knew she was not married to him. Unless—unless the man had been playing the role of husband too thoroughly, disgusting her with his ardor, although Alan would not have suspected that Ainsworth could act so hot-bloodedly.

Something had happened to send her hurtling down the stairs, something she wished to escape. Whatever it had been that had frightened her, she must know he would see that she would be safe with him.

"A nice attempt, Ainsworth—but it comes too late. Caroline has told me the truth," Alan said.

"Caroline?" Beatrix was standing at Edward's shoulder, having hurried into her clothing. Like him, she had grasped the seriousness of their situation at once, but was able to see a way out of their dilemma that she was certain had not occurred to him.

"This is what the doctor warned us about, Edward. The

poor girl's mind has snapped at last. Now, instead of going about the countryside, searching for the imaginary Caroline, she has come to think she *is* Caroline. Oh Edward, this is what I feared might happen if we took her away from the doctor's care too soon."

"Yes—my poor, dear April." He was immediately ready to follow Beatrix' lead once more. Their two stories could be combined and would be far more convincing when they were told together. The betrayed husband and the maddened wife. Who could doubt the truth of his charges, except Graves—and with all the servants to witness the scene which had just taken place, the man's role as the betrayer would be a most credible one.

"You are quite right, Bea. It was a dangerous thing to do to her; she was not ready to face the outside world. I can understand that now. Who knows what she might attempt next? We must see that she is confined, so that she can do no harm to herself or another."

He came several steps nearer to the pair and Alan put Caroline aside, facing Edward angrily. "No—you will not put her away somewhere while the pair of you enjoy my uncle's money."

"That was not—" Edward started.

Beatrix passed Edward and came to the foot of the stairs. "My poor April," she said in the caressing voice the girl had never heard from her since the day they left the doctor's surgery—and which she had found difficult to believe even before she knew the truth about the woman. "We should never have allowed you to do as much as you have. All this riding about . . . You have become ill again, as you were before—"

She put out a hand and Caroline shrank against Alan to escape it. She felt the woman's touch would be enough to draw her back under the other's spell, would contaminate her as she considered that the two of them were contaminated. Her only hope of freedom from that spell lay in the disgust she felt for the scene she had just witnessed. "No, do not touch me," she protested. "You—and your paramour—"

"Stark mad," Beatrix said sadly, letting her hand fall to

her side. "The advances this man has been making, added
to all those terrible things she saw in France have finally
unbalanced her, made her imagine things which have never
existed—"

"I have never been in France!" Caroline's voice rose to
a shriek. Beatrix shook her head, as if the hysterical voice
only proved her point.

"You see, Edward, this is just as the doctor warned us
might happen to one who suffers from her condition; she
has tried too hard to forget everything that happened, and
the result is that she has forgot you—and your part in her
life."

"The blame is mine," he said with feigned contriteness.
"I thought that bringing her here would help her, not destroy
her."

"I doubt that it would have done her any harm, if she
had not been seduced by this man," Beatrix continued. "We
ought to have left her safely with the doctor, as he asked us
to do, so that she could have recovered slowly—but how
could we know this would happen? Now I fear it is too late
even for him to save her, to restore her to sanity. Now she
not only wishes to deny the fact of her parents' death, but
of her marriage, as well."

"It will do you no good to say such things as that about
me because I know the truth now," Caroline said. She had
regained control of her voice, but she was unable to stop
herself from trembling. Would Alan—would anyone—believe her in the face of their calm statements that she had
gone mad?

Alan's arm was about her again, reassuring her of his love
and belief. "I think it is time for us to tell my uncle what
we know," he told her, leading her to the study. Edward
and Beatrix followed him closely, while Wilcox, suddenly
becoming aware of the interested footmen in the hallway,
ordered them back to their work.

Lord Hannaford looked up from the papers spread across
his desk, somewhat surprised at his nephew's entry without
having been announced, but more so at his being accompanied by the Ainsworths. The two men had customarily

avoided each other since their first meeting, and the older woman had openly sneered at Alan, accusing him of attempting to cheat his cousin of her rights.

Alan and Edward began speaking at once, but Hannaford silenced them with an upheld hand. "One at a time," he ordered, but before either of the men could say a word, Beatrix pushed her way past Edward, eager, as was her habit, to take control of the conversation.

"You should know, my lord, that your nephew has been responsible for a serious setback in my sister-in-law's condition."

"That is not true!" Caroline cried. "I am not the person—"

Edward stepped quickly to her side, catching her arm in attempt to prevent her from saying anything more. She pulled away from him and shrank against Alan, knowing she would be safe with him.

"You can see how it is, Your Lordship," Edward said. "I have just discovered that this man has been making love to my wife. I do not know how long such a state of affairs has been going on. Thinking he could be trusted, I have allowed her to ride out alone with him—and this is the result. And before the servants on this occasion; he had not even the decency to seek out somewhere private for his seduction." He was happy that Bea had used the word; it made what he must say so much more convincing.

"It was not—" Caroline began, but Edward would not allow her to finish.

"Doubtless this is not the first time it has happened," he repeated, and Caroline's flush when she remembered Alan's kiss upon the hilltop made it seem that he was right about her supposed infidelity.

"I had thought it safe to allow the pair of them to ride about the estate without my company," Edward continued. "And as a result of this—this attack on his part—she is so greatly overset by what has happened that she is attempting to convince herself that there is nothing wrong with her accepting his attentions or—"

"What my brother means to say—" Beatrix began.

"Let him speak for himself," Hannaford ordered. "He seems to be quite capable of doing so."

Beatrix scowled, but had no choice but to obey. She hoped that Edward could follow her lead. At least, it appeared that she had been wrong about his feelings for the chit; he might have admired her for a time, as he had done once before, but nothing could compare with his love for the earl's money—or for her.

"My sister was only attempting to help me. As you may imagine, I am extremely disturbed by the change in my wife's condition."

"I have never been his wife," Caroline protested. "I know that now. My name is Caroline—"

"Your Lordship has only to listen to her to see what has occurred. In her attempt to convince herself that there was nothing evil in this man's designs upon her virtue, she has now told herself that she is not my wife, but the Caroline for whom her poor mind has been seeking. I feared something of the kind might happen, and was planning to take her to the seashore. It was my hope that the change of scene might help her."

"You have already given her a great many changes of scene if your stories have been true—which we know they have not been. If none of them have been of any benefit, why should you think another change would help her?" Alan wanted to know.

"Be quiet!" Lord Hannaford ordered. "There will be no trips to the seashore or anywhere until this matter has been cleared up to my satisfaction."

"You are right, of course," Edward agreed in a sad tone. He would not defy the earl—at least, not openly. There were far better ways of dealing with the matter. "Besides, I fear it is now too late for anything of that sort to help her. Her mania has now reached the stage where I cannot see any other choice but to have her confined, although I should be heartbroken to do so. Who knows what damage she might do to herself—or to others?"

"That will not be done, either, unless it is done by my order. The young woman—whether she is my granddaughter or some other—will remain here, as will the pair of you. And you," the earl turned to his nephew, "will not exchange so much as a word with her unless I say that you may do so. Is that understood?"

"But, Lord Hannaford—" Caroline began.

"And you will not make any attempt to have any dealings with him again. You will remain here with your husband and his sister."

"But I am trying to tell you that they are not my husband and—"

"April, dear—" Beatrix began.

"I am *not* April! And I am not the one you should be calling 'dear.' Everyone will soon know that you are not Edward's sister, but his paramour."

Rather than displaying the anger Caroline thought to evoke by her charge, anger which might cause the other to speak rashly, the older woman shook her head sadly. "You can see for yourself the pitiful state she is in," she said to the earl. "The doctor warned us that something of this kind might happen if the poor child became overset. And your nephew's attentions . . . After all, he is her cousin, and she is a married woman—"

"No! I am not!"

Lord Hannaford came to Caroline's side and put a protective arm about her shoulders. "You must not worry yourself about any of this," he told her. "All will be be well. I shall summon my own physician and he will give you something to soothe you."

"No!" Caroline shouted again, pulling away from him and throwing herself into Alan's arms. "Do not let them do this to me. They will take me away while I am asleep—lock me up as a madwoman. You know I am telling the truth."

"I know that you are, but you must not fear my uncle's physician. He is a good man, and will not condemn you as they are doing. In the meantime—"

"In the meantime, Alan, you will stay far from the girl— or I shall send you away," the earl said sternly.

"No—do not do that," Caroline pleaded. "I shall not speak to him until you say that I may do so."

"Very well. Let us forget about that for now." Once more Hannaford placed his arm about her shoulders. "And you, my child, can come to me whenever you like. We can talk about what oversets you."

Chapter Sixteen

Caroline did not see the glance Lord Hannaford exchanged over her head with Edward, but Alan was fully aware of it and sensed the possible danger to his beloved. Upon thought, his uncle might come to agree with the others that Caroline was in need of care. They might be permitted to take her away before he could do anything to help her. He resolved that, regardless of any promise Caroline had been forced to make to avoid him, he would somehow manage to speak to her as soon as he could reach her without stirring up his uncle's wrath against both of them.

There was no doubt in his mind that Hannaford would do as he threatened and immediately exile him from Silver Acres if he had the slightest suspicion of any clandestine meeting between them. What was worse, he might then allow that pair of tricksters to take the girl away with them in order to keep her out of his way.

She had been able to tell him so little about herself in the few moments between the time he had gathered her up from her fall on the stairs, to learn that she had regained her memory, and Edward's coming down from whatever had occurred upstairs to make his accusation against the

173

pair of them. Unless he was given more information abou
her background, the name of someone who could vouc
for her, there was nothing he could do to help her.

Beatrix and Edward traded troubled glances. Would th
girl say anything to his lordship about what she had seen i
the bedroom, about the scene which had set her to flight
Her words had sounded so wild that she had played into the
hands the few times she had been permitted to speak.

By making their accusations of madness against her s
quickly, they had managed to prevent her saying anythin
more about them at present, but what of the future? If sh
should talk to the earl, should tell what she had discovere
about them, would they still be able to convince the ol
man that all of this was nothing more than another produc
of her disordered imagination?

"Do you think it possible that this latest fall may hav
been enough to make her forget what had occurred?" Edwar
asked anxiously.

Beatrix bit her lip and shook her head at that. April'
remark about a paramour made it evident to her that th
girl must have remembered at least a part of what had take
place, but at present, she had not been able to convinc
the earl that she was telling the truth about anything, eve
about her name. They had been able to explain away he
accusations as the ravings of a disturbed mind.

"At least," Beatrix murmured as they made their way u
the stairs, "she has not yet had an opportunity to *say* any
thing—nothing more than that one remark about us. An
it sounded too wild—"

"I doubt that anything she has said has been enough
make the old man think you and I are scheming to get ou
hands on April's inheritance," Edward agreed. "If we ca
only prevent her from confiding further in him."

"We know that she certainly has told Graves whatever sh
suspects about us, but Lord Hannaford will not be so quic
to believe her, even if she does tell him what she saw. Too
it may be that now that she knows once more who she i
she will soon forget everything that happened in between
No one can know how such things may develop, so we ca

ope it will come to that. And if there is an opportunity for
s to get her away from here—"

Edward nodded. "Yes—we must do something about her
uickly, before she is able to convince the earl that she is
ot merely raving when she spins her tale about not being
April."

"She is certain to do so, of course, if he permits her to say
anything more than she has already done. For the present,
do not believe he is in the mood to do so, but we must
ct without delay, before he does attempt to question her
gain."

"Of course, Bea—you are right, as always. Although
ow we are to get her away from here when he is willing
o shelter her, I cannot see. And what shall we do about
his physician he wishes to call? He may say that she is
ow telling the truth."

"How can he do that?" Her tone was scornful. "He knows
othing whatever about the girl, so there is nothing he can
ay about her, save that her health is good. And that, we
lready know."

"Yes, but about her mind—her memory—" Edward
egan.

"There is no way for him to tell if she is mad or sane. You
ust remember that her tale is so fantastic that it is doubtful
nyone will put any stock in it—except Graves, of course."

"*He* believes everything she has said; I am certain of that.
ou must have heard what he was saying when we came
own the stairs. What if he is able to convince the old man
hat she is telling the truth?" There was a hint of panic in
dward's voice.

"Yes, he believes her; it was only to be expected that he
would do so. We know the fool is in love with her. But we
an discount him, claiming that he pretends to believe her
o get her away from you," Beatrix said soothingly. "We
now, too, that he does not dare do anything against the
ld man's orders for fear of being sent away from here. As
ong as we do not lose our heads . . . "

Caroline had lingered after the others left, hoping for an
pportunity to tell her tale to the old man. Beatrix had been

right about him, however—he was in no mood to listen to
her until he had an opportunity to go over the various stories
more thoroughly. He merely patted her shoulder and told
her she was not to worry about anything. "I shall see that
you are not taken away from here," he promised.

"At least, that much is good," she told herself; but she
could not help the feeling that all else had been lost. Now
that she knew who she was, knew that she had the right to
love Alan, she was forbidden even to see him, to ask for
his help. And she feared she would need it, for if the earl
could not be convinced to believe her, she did not feel she
was strong enough to fight the others alone.

What if Beatrix and Edward—she was certain, as she had
been from the beginning, that it was Beatrix who was the
guiding member of the pair—were able to convince Lord
Hannaford that she had truly gone mad, and that Alan was
to blame for her present state?

"If they can convince him of that, the earl may—no, he
almost certainly *will* send Alan away for as long as I am
allowed to remain here. That would be a horrible fate for
him, considering how deeply he loves Silver Acres," she
whispered as she stumbled up to her room. "What can I do
to help him, except to stay away from him as I have been
ordered to do?"

On the other hand, since Alan was his heir, his lordship
might prefer not to exile him. Rather, despite what he had
just promised her, he might permit Edward and Beatrix to
take her away. Away to some madhouse—or worse. She
knew they would not—could not—permit her to convince
anyone that she was now telling the truth about their scheme;
they would do whatever was needed to stop her from talking.
All of their plans to obtain a share of Lord Hannaford's
fortune now depended upon having her accepted as a mad
woman.

Of course, the earl *had* told her that she would not be
taken from here, and she hoped she could depend upon his
word for that, no matter what the others might say about
her. But even if he insisted that she should stay on the estate,
there was no way of being certain that he would not agree

o have her confined in one of the upper rooms, doubtless
with a lock on the door and bars upon the windows, lest
he escape and harm herself.

She doubted that the disturbed state of her mind—as his
ordship would be convinced to see it—would have any
ffect upon the inheritance. Lord Hannaford would feel
hat it was more than ever necessary to provide for her, and
would merely see that Edward was named to administer the
state for her.

He and Beatrix would have what they wanted. They
would have won—and what would become of her? Sooner
r later, the pair of them would have to find a way to dispose
f her, lest the earl somehow become convinced she was
elling the truth.

She sat at the window, toying with the tassel of the
rape while these thoughts went around in her mind until
he feared she *would* go mad trying to solve her problem.
A light scratching at the door startled her, then Lucy slipped
nto the room.

"I daren't stay more than a moment," she whispered.
Mrs. Armstrong says that since you haven't no need of
me just now, she wants me to help her with some household
asks. And Miss Ainsworth says I must do as she tells me.
think 'tis her way of keeping me away from you, though
he did not say as much and I do not know why she should
ct this way." *Except,* she said to herself, *that the old cat
ishes to punish me for being loyal to my mistress.* "But
slipped away to give you . . . " She held out a twist of
aper.

Caroline snatched it from her and untwisted it to read:
My love, you did not have an opportunity to tell me the
ame of your last employer. If I can see her, she will cer-
ainly be able to prove to my Uncle's satisfaction that you
re not April Ainsworth." There was no signature, but none
was needed. There was only one person on whom she could
epend. *Two,* she amended silently, for she knew she could
ust Lucy. But only Alan could help her.

"My love." Caroline mentally treasured the phrase, but
he rest of the message made her frown. When she left Mrs.

Logan's house, she had determined she would put the wom
an's angry remarks from her mind. Now the mere though
of her former employer was enough to bring them back i
force. *Would* the woman be willing to come to her aid—c
would she be so spiteful as to refuse to do anything for her

"After all," Caroline whispered, not willing even for Luc
to know the truth about her last position, "it was not my fau
that young Simon Logan had cornered me in the schoolroor
that day. And his mother knew that, well enough, whe
she found us there—she knew about the reputation he ha
acquired, despite his youth, knew also that there was n
way I could defend myself against one who was almos
twice my size, even if he was six years younger than I
It was only her arrival that saved me." But of course, th
woman *would* say that her son could do no wrong and
would be the governess who was blamed in such a case.

"Still, I must hope she will tell that I was with her. Tha
should be enough to convince the earl," she murmured
then, catching the maid's curious glance said, "Can yo
wait a moment or two until I write an answer?"

Lucy nodded and Caroline went to her desk, scribbling
note as quickly as possible. As she gave it to the girl, Luc
said, "Is it true that you are not Mrs. Ainsworth, after all?

"Yes—but it would be best if you said nothing about tha
before the other servants," she advised.

The word would go around the household quickly enoug
if Lord Hannaford accepted her story and sent her away. I
he was willing to permit Beatrix and Edward to have thei
way, she would still be "married," but would be though
mad. Everyone would know that, too.

For the moment, however, it would be the wisest cours
to have no gossip spread about her. If such a thing was sti
possible, when so many of the servants had overheard a
least a part of their quarrel.

"Oh, I can keep mum," Lucy promised. "No need fo
you to worry about me, you know that. Some of the other
are talking, but they know nothing for certain. But wha
will you do about those two?" She nodded in the directio
of the other's rooms. "Will *they* be quiet?"

"Yes—about that, at least. Neither of them will say anything about who I am, for it is to their advantage not to own that the tale of my marriage was a fraud. As to the rest, I have no way of knowing what they will do, Lucy—except that I think they hope to have me declared mad."

"Oh, Madam—Miss—they cannot do that! 'Tis never true!"

"Do you think they will hesitate at another lie—now? I hope Mr. Graves can do something."

"Oh, I know he will help you." Lucy had formed a strong admiration for the young gentleman, and thought it would be a wonderful thing if he could take the lady far away from these people who were being so cruel to her. If only the two of them could be happy together.

"I hope he can do so," Caroline said. "Now, you had best return below stairs before anyone suspects you have come up here. You know how Beatrix is, always going about, trying to find something for which I can be blamed. If she suspected you were carrying a message to Mr. Graves for me, she would take it to his lordship, and Alan—Mr. Graves—would be sent away from Silver Acres. Then there would be no one who could help me."

Lucy scurried away with the precious bit of paper, but found no opportunity to slip it into Alan Graves' hand that evening as he sauntered through the kitchen and stopped to exchange a word with the cook, hoping for a chance to talk to the young maid. The housekeeper, doubtless prompted by Miss Ainsworth, saw to it that Lucy was kept busy while young Mr. Graves was there.

In desperation, Lucy slipped away for a moment to see her young footman. "Please, Edward," she begged, "I need your help. 'Tis most important that this be given to Mr. Graves when no one can see you."

"What business do you have, writing notes to the likes of him?" the young man demanded jealously.

"Idiot! Why should I write him—even if I knew how, which I never learned? 'Tis a message from my mistress—and the old dragon would like nothing better than to hear of it."

He studied her for a moment, still suspicious, but in company with most of the servants, he had felt the sharp edge of Miss Ainsworth's tongue, while the younger lady had always been kind to him, especially since he had been seeing Lucy whenever he could do so. "All right," he promised. "Trust me to see he gets it."

"And see the old cat does not find out about it."

"Never you mind about that. I think I can do what is necessary," the footman said.

It was some time before he was able to make an excuse to get away so he could take the message to the impatient young gentleman. "Lucy says 'tis from her mistress," he reported. He had heard some of the uproar this afternoon and wondered what part Mr. Graves had played in it. Had he truly driven the lady mad, as some of the others were saying? It did not seem to be the sort of thing Mr. Graves would do to anyone, especially to a nice lady like Miss April.

To his pleased surprise, the gentleman seized the paper and slipped a coin into his hand. "Use a part of it to get your Lucy a new riband or something of the sort."

"Yes sir, and thank you, sir." He had caught the glint of gold in his palm before the coin was deftly slipped from sight. As much as the pair of them might earn in half a year. Mr. Graves was a true gentleman. Whatever they were saying about him could not be so.

When he had read the message, Alan went at once to his lordship. "I should like your permission, Uncle, to be away from the estate for several weeks," he said. "It is a matter of some importance."

With a grim smile, the earl agreed that it might be well for the young man to go—to "take care of the important matter." This was only an excuse, Hannaford told himself, for his nephew to take himself as far from temptation's way as was possible. At least, for the present. And that would be the best thing he could do.

Although he would not have said it to anyone, Hannaford confessed to himself that there were a great number of things about this Ainsworth affair which still puzzled him. For one thing, it was totally unlike Alan to involve himself with married female, especially one who was living beneath his uncle's roof.

He did not doubt there were any number of married ladies who would welcome such a liaison, especially with his heir—but his granddaughter certainly would not do so. Or was the girl actually not his granddaughter, after all, as she was now declaring? And if she were not April, how did she happen to be married to Ainsworth? And where was his granddaughter, if not here?

Was the tale of the marriage, too, a fiction, as she had appeared to be trying to say? And was Alan in some way responsible for her sudden declaration that she was *not* his granddaughter, after all the trouble the trio had taken to convince him of the sincerity of her claim? He shook his head over the impossibility of understanding all of this.

"Not that I should begrudge the lad a bit of dalliance now and then," Hannaford said to himself, looking after his nephew as he left the study. "But this is not the place for it. Doubtless he has been spending too much time on the estate since Arthur died. It will do him good to get about, meet a number of nice—or not so nice—females, and come back cured of his *tendre* for the girl, whoever she may prove to be."

Alan, however, had no intention of behaving as his uncle thought he intended to do. He estimated that he would have a three-days' ride to the tiny Sussex village Caroline had given as her employer's home, but found himself longer on the road than that.

This was not far from one of the Hannaford estates, one that might well have been given to April, if she were alive. Alan had never had an opportunity to visit this particular estate, so he was not acquainted with the area. Twice, when he had stopped to ask directions from the natives, what he had been told led him far afield and he was forced to retrace his path, wondering if the country-folk he met knew one-half as much about their neighborhood as they pretended.

When at last he had reached his destination, the timidity of the maidservant who ran to fetch her mistress made him happy Caroline no longer worked there. His first glimpse

of the gaunt, grim-faced female and her sharp demand to
be told his business made him certain he was correct.

"May I enquire, Madam, if you have recently had a Miss
Caroline Kingston in your employ?"

"That hussy!" Her voice became shrill. "Throwing out
her lures to an innocent boy—yes, she was here. But not
for long, I can tell you that much, as soon as I learned the
truth about her. I would wager she is causing more trouble
wherever she is."

"I should not say that she was exactly causing trouble,
Mrs. Logan—but that she has become the victim of a plot,"
Alan said. "I have learned she has fallen afoul of a pair of
treacherous individuals."

"More like, she was the ringleader. I hope she swings
for whatever she has done."

"I do not believe that it will go as badly as that for any
of them, but there will doubtless be prison sentences await-
ing the guilty parties when they have been brought to justice."

"We-ell, that would be better than nothing, I suppose,"
Mrs. Logan conceded. "But it is too bad if they will not
all hang. Especially that Kingston trollop."

"That may be. But whatever their fate is to be, you can
be of considerable help in bringing them to justice. There is
a pair of adventurers who have been attempting to convince
my uncle that Miss Kingston is his missing granddaughter,
a young lady named April Ainsworth. Would you be willing to return with me to Silver Acres and tell him who she
actually is?"

"I have never heard of any such place." *And if I have not
heard of it, it must not exist,* her manner appeared to say.
"And I know every place within a score of miles of here.
That means it would be a journey of some distance from
here, would it not?"

"Yes—it would take us several days to arrive there. Not
as long as it took me to come here, since I now know the
way. However, I should be willing to undertake all of your
expenses—post charges, lodging, meals, and whatever is
necessary."

Mrs. Logan gave him a sharp glance. "To be willing to pay out so much as such places charge, it must be worth your while to have me come with you."

"It would." Alan had heard that tone before. It seemed she was greedy, as well as vindictive. That could be used to advantage—or at least, he hoped it would be an advantage. It was difficult to imagine so tiny a girl having been a governess, and he could never have been made to believe that Caroline could have been guilty of attempting to seduce a schoolboy.

If that was this woman's opinion of her, however, would it help or hurt his darling's cause to take so abusive a person to Silver Acres? He had no wish to cause Caroline further unhappiness—but if he could not help her to prove her true identity, that pernicious pair might well have her committed to Bedlam while they were free to enjoy his uncle's money.

"Naturally," he continued, feeling that he would give up the entire estate if it were necessary in order to obtain the information Caroline needed so badly. "I should be willing also to make some reasonable contribution—doubtless, you will have to arrange for someone to care for your home while you are away."

"Oh, the servants can manage—" She caught herself quickly at the thought of a "reasonable contribution." That might earn her as much as ten pounds, as well as having him pay all the expenses of her journey. And that for venting her spite on the Kingston female.

"You are right, of course; I will need to engage someone to oversee their work while I am away from home. Servants are such lazy creatures; one can never depend upon them to do what they should unless there is someone to look over their shoulders every moment. You must know how it is."

"Oh, certainly, Madam." Alan knew well what she had in mind, but was willing to do what was necessary.

"And then, there is the matter of my little daughter's welfare and education to consider," Mrs. Logan continued. "I have employed a new governess for her, but who knows how the woman might behave while I am away? She might allow the child to fritter away her time."

At least, she told herself, she had persuaded the school authorities to accept Simon once more, so there would be no more trouble on that head. She had also warned the boy that another such report from the school authorities would result in her stopping his allowance. He knew his mother well enough to know that while she would turn a blind eye toward his escapades, anything which might cost her money would be viewed quite differently.

Should he return while she was away, she knew that not even he would have been tempted to any indiscretion by the vinegary spinster she had employed to take Miss Kingston's place. She would never have admitted it to anyone, but Mrs. Logan held herself to blame in a way for what had happened; she should have known better than to employ the young woman in the first place, but how was she to know that Simon would be sent down?

Alan doubted she would engage anyone to look after the place or to supervise her daughter's schooling while she was away. That was merely a ploy to get more money from him. "Shall we say one hundred pounds?" he suggested.

"One hun—" She stared at him for an instant, then made a quick recover, wondering how much more she might persuade him to pay. "And the expenses of my journey."

"Certainly."

"Then I shall go. Someone should denounce the girl."

Caroline, am I helping you or hurting you by bringing this creature to Silver Acres? Alan asked himself, as he counted out the bills, then, on a sudden thought, returned them to his pocket. "They will be yours," he told her, "as soon as you have identified the young lady."

Chapter Seventeen

Long before they had reached Silver Acres, Alan had confirmed the far from pleasant opinion of Mrs. Logan he had formed when they first met. She complained constantly to the coachman: he was either traveling much too slowly which wasted time and good money, or too recklessly—they were certain to be overturned.

Had the man not been in her employ, Alan had no doubt he would have left them driverless the first time they stopped to change horses. He only marveled that the driver had not long ago found a more congenial place to work. Whatever he might be paid—and Alan doubted the woman would pay more than she was forced to do—it could not be enough to make up for being forced to accept such abuse day after day. If he were driving so that he would strike the rougher parts of the road by design, Alan silently cheered him on, and hoped for more uneven roads ahead.

Whenever the horses were changed, the new ones were never more to the lady's taste than were the habits of her coachman. They were far too mettlesome and might be expected to run away with the carriage and wreck it, or else they were mere sluggards, causing them to waste time which might be better spent—in what manner it might be spent, she did not specify, but gave the impression that her time was valuable indeed. If she could find nothing else wrong, it seemed that the various animals of a team were refusing to pull together, which caused the carriage to lurch about, so that she was continually nauseated by the movement.

The road tolls were exorbitant, and she was certain they were collected far too often—although Alan, and not she, was paying them. Also, she told Alan repeatedly that whatever lodgings he found for them were completely unfit for human occupancy, and that he was being greatly overcharged for the inferior service they received.

Doubtless, he decided, had the lady—and he used the term advisedly—not had the excuse of her son's pursuit of the governess, she would soon have found some other reason to discharge her. A girl who was as lovely as Caroline must have suffered a great many insults under the domination of such a tigress.

Whatever the reason for her leaving the Logan household, he could only be happy for the girl that she was no longer at the beck of this virago—not that he considered her present situation with Beatrix to be much better. But he reminded himself all would change when Hannaford had learned the truth about her—and about the pair of scoundrels who were calling themselves her family.

If only I could arrange to have Mrs. Logan quarrel with Beatrix Ainsworth when we arrive home, he thought. *I wonder which of them would be the victor in such a skirmish— or would they end by demolishing each other?* The idea of so pleasant a culmination to all of their troubles was enough to set him to whistling as he rode alongside the carriage.

"Young man," Mrs. Logan shouted, leaning from the window of her carriage. "Stop that racket at once. You are giving me a severe migraine."

"Yes, Madam," Alan said, exchanging grimaces with the driver. Both were certain that she could not have heard a note of his whistling over the sound of the wheels upon the rocky road. His enjoyment of the day was only another thing about which she could complain.

He winked at the driver, then pursed his mouth as if whistling, but without making a sound. Moments later, Mrs. Logan again issued a command for him to stop making so much noise. He and the driver grinned at one another at this evidence that she was animadverting without knowing whether she had a reason to do so.

Only the sight of Silver Acres silenced her complaints for some moments. Alan supposed she was thinking that one who lived in so fine a place would have been willing to give her more money for coming to his aid. He would have done so, had it been necessary to induce her to come, but reflected that he had already, for no more than a few days of her time, certainly offered her many times the amount of a governess' yearly wage.

"Will you ask my uncle if he will see us, Wilcox?" Alan asked after he had assisted Mrs. Logan from her carriage. "And ask the Ainsworths if they will join us in the study?"

Wilcox looked at the woman as if he thought she should have come to the kitchen door, but replied, "Certainly, Mr. Graves."

Before the butler was out of range of her voice, Mrs. Logan said, "High and mighty, ain't he? Far too much so for a servant, if you was to ask me. In *my* house, you can be certain the servants know their place."

I have no doubt of that, Alan said to himself, recalling the intimidated maidservant and the woman's unending abuse of the driver and of himself. Knowing a grin would doubtless add to her anger, he kept all expression from his face as he said aloud, "We have never had any qualms about Wilcox. He never forgets that he is in the service of a peer of the realm, and has always behaved accordingly."

"You mean *royalty*?"

Was she truly so ignorant as that, or was she merely overwhelmed by the size of the estate? "We can hardly claim to be among the rulers of the kingdom, but my Uncle is the fifth Earl of Hannaford."

"An earl, is he? Then it should have been worth more

to him to have me come here."

"I doubt that indeed, Madam—but we can ask him about the matter, if you like."

"Back so soon?" Hannaford asked when the pair entered his study. As the butler had done, he cast a disparaging eye upon Alan's companion. "I am surprised to see you; I had not expected you to return for some weeks. And, tell me, Alan—is this the best you were able to do for yourself while you were away? Perhaps you should have taken the time to look about you more carefully."

Mrs. Logan glared at him. "You may be an earl," she snapped, "or you may not—I have only this man's word for that, and I do not know what it is worth. I found him to be undependable in so many ways during our journey that I would not know if he lied to me."

All thought of making any attempt to get a larger "contribution" from this haughty gentleman had left her at his words. She could see that he was the mifty sort who might even refuse to permit the younger man to give her the money she had been promised for coming here.

No matter how high he was, however, he had no right to speak of her as he had done, as if she were a Nobody. "But if he *is* telling the truth and you *are* an earl, that does not mean that you can insult a lady."

Looking at his nephew, who was fighting to restrain a grin at having his uncle so addressed—for this set down did much to recompense him for the many insults she had given him while they were on the road—the earl said solemnly, "You are quite right, Madam. I must ask your pardon for my rudeness. But what brings you to Silver Acres?"

The woman opened her mouth to give him her opinion of the girl she was to identify, but, knowing what she would say, Alan quickly forestalled her.

"This lady, Uncle, is Mrs. Logan, who, until recently, was the employer of Miss Caroline Kingston, a governess. She has gone to a great deal of trouble," the eye farthest from her closed in a wink, "to come with me to identify the young lady who has been presented to you as April Ainsworth."

"Lady? You call her a lady?" Mrs. Logan took this opportunity to begin her tirade. "That—"

"Yes—you have told me what you think of her. Many times. But why do we not wait? The Ainsworths should be here in a moment."

Almost as he uttered the words, Wilcox rapped upon the door and announced, "Mr. and Mrs. Ainsworth and Miss Ainsworth, as you requested, Mr. Graves."

"Oh, so you are the one who has been putting us to such trouble, are you?" Beatrix said angrily. "Had we known it was you, we should not have come down. After all, the earl has forbid you to annoy our poor April further. And he was right to do so, for look what trouble you have caused for her with your philandering. And what anguish you have caused my poor Edward, as well. What business do you think you have in summoning us?"

"I thought it might be a good notion to have you meet someone," Alan told her. "The way in which the two of you are lingering in the doorway, one would think that you felt yourselves in peril. There is no need for you to adopt such caution—at least, until you have heard me out. Will you not come in, Miss Ainsworth—if that is who you are, which I must confess that I doubt—and become acquainted with Mrs. Logan? I am certain she is already familiar with the young lady you are attempting to pass off to my uncle as April."

He reached out a hand to Caroline, who took it gladly. "Oh yes, I know Mrs. Logan, and she knows me. Do you not, ma'am?"

"Yes I know you—only too well, I am sorry to say. You, who enticed my poor boy—"

Alan squeezed Caroline's hand encouragingly as she replied with some spirit, "You know quite well, Mrs. Logan, that it was your 'poor boy,' as you choose to call him, who was at fault on that occasion, one which I understand was not a new one to him. Had he not already been expelled from college for his entanglement with a—"

"That is quite enough of that," the woman said hastily, unwilling to have her son's peccadillos made more public than they already had been. "And besides, they have taken him back, which proves he was innocent all the time and the charge naught but a hoax, designed to get more money from me. Not that they succeeded, I may tell you, for I am not one to be choused out of my hard-earned pence. You wished me to tell you that I recognize this person," she said to Alan. "Well, I do so—I know all about her. To my sorrow. And whatever may be done to her for attempting to force herself upon your family is well deserved."

"Thank you, Mrs. Logan, that is all we wished from you. I am certain you must be eager to return home, as you told me—in some detail—that your servants were badly in need of someone to watch them and make certain they do not skimp any of their chores, and that you also were uncertain about the ability of your new governess to care for your daughter. After all, you had no chance to find such a person before we set out."

"That is all well and good, Mr. Graves, and perhaps I may have said something which led you to think that," Mrs. Logan replied, having been permitted to glimpse at least a part of the grandeur of Silver Acres and thinking how proud she would be if she could tell her friends that she had been invited to remain here—if only for a night.

She could wander about the place during the night, when there was no one watching her, to see more of its treasures. Perhaps she might pocket one or two small items which would not be missed in all this splendor. A few souvenirs to prove to all that she had truly been here, she told herself, although such trinkets might bring in a pretty penny after she had impressed her friends with them. It was an opportunity which might never come her way again.

"But I see no need for me to make such haste as all that to return to them," she insisted. "They will do well enough without me for another day or two, I have no doubt. And I do not consider it advisable to begin a journey so late in the day. Who knows what a body might encounter upon the road, once it becomes dark?"

Alan was equally determined that the woman should not remain here for so much as a moment more than was necessary to resolve this business. Also, he thought that any brigand who met this virago upon the road must look to his own safety.

"Ah, but you must remember," he told her, "that it will take you several days of traveling to reach your home, and I know you would not wish to take the risk of something going amiss merely because you had not arrived home in time to oversee them."

Alan had a firm hand beneath her elbow and was guiding her out the door, despite her continued protest than she could see no good reason why she should leave in so great a hurry. She could scarcely drag her feet, and so was forced to go forward as he wished. To the waiting butler, he said, "Wilcox, you will please see to it that Mrs. Logan has whatever you may need for her return home."

"Whatever you say, Mr. Graves," the man said, thinking that were the matter left up to him, he would dismiss the coachman and leave the beldam to walk home.

"And what about my—" Mrs. Logan began.

"And when you are certain she is leaving," Alan interrupted, "not before, you may give her this." A roll of notes slipped into Wilcox's hand. "And this," a smaller amount joined the first, "you may give to the coachman to defray the expenses of the journey." He was too wise to permit that portion of the money to fall into her miserly hands, lest she starve both horses and driver.

Mrs. Logan began still another protest, but Wilcox was well accustomed to handling obstreperous people. He had heard her description of him, and ushered her out the door and into her carriage before any other words were half-spoken. "I wish you a pleasant journey, Madam," he told her as he closed the door firmly, much too polite to voice his true animosity toward one who had been under his master's roof, no matter what the reason for her coming.

"What about my—" The notes which the man placed in her hand were enough to silence the remainder of her protest as she began to count them carefully, determined she would not leave Silver Acres until she was certain she had received everything she had been promised. The money was all there—and she thought herself a fool for not having insisted upon more when she had first been urged to come here with him. The young gudgeon would doubtless have given her as much as she wished to see that she identified that hussy of a governess.

"Although why he should take so much bother for her, I cannot tell," she muttered. "But men are ever such idiots for a pretty face." She recalled how foolishly Simon had behaved about the creature. . . .

Still, she had her hundred pounds, which was more than she had expected when he had first suggested the journey, and she did not doubt that she could contrive to save a bit out of the funds her coachman had received, by staying in cheaper lodgings and changing horses less often. That was what she would do, if only she could force him to turn the money over to her—but with so much in his hands, the man might desert her at their first halt. The young idiot should have known better than to entrust money to a servant. That was the trouble with nobs like him—they had no idea of the value of a pound.

As she thought that, her carriage lurched and began down the long drive.

Returning to the study, Alan said to Caroline, "I must apologize to you, my dear, for having subjected you to her presence, for I learned on our journey how she must have persecuted you. But I was certain she could verify your story that you are not Mrs. April Ainsworth. As to whether you are Mrs. anyone else, I am inclined to take your word upon that subject."

"Oh, I knew she would act horribly—she was never any other way to those in her employ—but I could not think of anyone else you could find so quickly who would tell you the truth about me, at least, about who I am." She supposed Mrs. Logan had not lost the opportunity to tell Alan her tale about the matter of young Simon, but he did not behave as if he had believed it.

"I trust, Uncle," he was saying to Hannaford, "you are willing now to believe that Caroline is truly who she claims to be."

The earl nodded. "I have been certain of that fact for
•me time."

"So that is how it is," Beatrix exclaimed, quick to see
at their earlier tales would no longer be of use, and that
•mething far different would be needed if they were to
ve themselves. "The chit has managed to trick us, and
›u, as well. She came to us in London and hired Edward
›d myself to pretend we knew she was April Ainsworth
›d that Edward was her husband. I own that it sounded
•mewhat havey-cavey to us at the time, but how were we
know that she was an imposter?"

"I see." Hannaford nodded, as if believing every word
eatrix spoke. "And what have you to say about the docu-
ents Mr. Ainsworth presented as proof of his tale?"

"Forged, I have no doubt, although they appeared to be
:nuine when she gave them to us. But how should we
ıow about such things? She must have had someone who
›uld make up such papers for her, for a price. I have heard
ere are such persons."

Edward nodded, willing, as before, to allow Beatrix to
ke the lead. Bea was always the wise one. Who else could
ıve thought as quickly as she of a way they might still be
›le to lay the blame at the girl's door and thus extricate
emselves from their dilemma?

"I do not doubt that you have heard of them," the earl
ıid to her. "But of course, *you* have never made use of
ıch creatures."

"Certainly, I have not." Her tone was indignant. "Why
ıould I do so?"

"For no reason that I know." His own tone was bland, as
he had merely mentioned such a fact in passing. "Now if
understand you correctly, you are telling me that the pair
` you is entirely innocent of any sort of wrongdoing—
cept, of course, of having been this young lady's witting
:complices in an attempt to defraud me."

"As I told you, we were merely hired to play our parts,"
eatrix said. "We had no way of knowing that her tale
as not true. Except, of course, for the part about Edward
:ing her husband—but she explained that she had need

of a gentleman to present her story to you, as it would b
unlike that you would listen to a female."

"That is not so, none of it," Caroline exclaimed. "I nev
saw either of these people until I woke in the doctor's su
gery and saw *her* leaning over me, saying that she was m
husband's sister and that the two of them had been searchir
for me."

"I do not doubt she was telling the truth about that mucl
my dear, if about nothing else we have heard here," the ea
reassured her. "The pair must have been in dire need, b
that time, of finding someone who could play the part c
my granddaughter. You must be about the proper age—
and since you did not know who you were or what ha
happened to you, you were the ideal choice for the role."

"You are making a preposterous charge," Beatrix pr
tested.

"Do you think so? Then what would you call the state
ments you have been making about Miss Kingston? Yc
forget that when you first arrived here, I told you that I ha
certain ways of checking upon the validity of the papers yc
brought, despite the turmoil in France at the present time.
have done so." Hannaford turned to his desk and picked u
a sheaf of papers.

Beatrix and Edward exchanged uneasy glances. True—
he had told them he could check their stories, but they ha
not thought it possible for him to do so, at least, before h
had settled a part of his fortune upon the girl. After all, th
papers were genuine, and with Edward's story there migl
have been no reason for the earl to check any further. Ar
if he should attempt to do so, there was so much unrest i
France at present there was a chance that he might neve
receive a reply.

"Rather than the claim you made to me earlier, that c
having married my granddaughter in France so that yc
could bring her to me, you now say the pair of you wer
inveigled into this plot by the young woman who has no
been identified as Caroline Kingston."

"No—" Caroline began, but the earl silenced her with
wave of his hand.

"That is quite correct, Your Lordship," Edward said. He depended upon Bea to rescue them from this imbroglio, and was content to follow her lead.

"And you and this other lady are truly brother and sister?"

Recalling the scene the girl had witnessed in the bedroom and fearing that she might blurt out something about it to the earl, Beatrix said, "No, Your Lordship, that is not quite true. Edward and I have been married for several years."

Chapter Eighteen

Caroline gasped and took a step nearer to Alan as if she felt that Beatrix' announcement meant further danger to her. He placed his arm about her and murmured in her ear, "Do not worry, dear one. You can safely leave everything in uncle's hands now, as he said."

"No, Madam," Hannaford was saying to Beatrix. "This man is neither your brother nor your husband. I sent accurate descriptions of both of you to my agent in Paris. His reply is that you," he nodded toward Edward, "are truly the man you claimed to be when you came here, and that you were married to my granddaughter April."

"Then that much was true," Caroline said. "After all I have heard from them, I should not have believed . . . Then why did he—?"

"But I am sorry to say that I have been informed the truth of Mr. Ainsworth's story ends there," the earl continued. "My man reports, sir, that April Ainsworth—*my granddaughter*—died under most suspicious circumstances, as a result of which the French authorities are quite anxious to speak to you and your—paramour. I believe that is how Miss Kingston referred to her during your last confrontation, is it not? It is as good a description of the woman as any."

"Lies! Nothing but a tissue of lies!" Beatrix shouted. "There is not a word of truth in that tale. Or if there is, it has nothing to do with either of us. Edward's name is not Ainsworth, but Johnston, and I am his wife. Neither of us has ever been to France, nor had we heard the name Ainsworth until this female employed us—"

"A likely tale, this new one, is it not, Uncle?" Alan asked, grinning at the earl. "Did I not tell you they were imposters?"

"Nothing of the kind," Beatrix protested. "We are—"

Edward sighed. "It is no good attempting to go on, Bea. As quick as you are, you can never convince them now; if the man in Paris has identified—"

"He did so, and to be certain that there was no error, he also sent sketches of the pair of you which the French police had in their files, as well as the description of you which was circulated when the search for you began. There is no possible chance of your having been mistaken for two other people."

He showed several sketches to Alan, who examined them, compared them with the pair standing before him, nodded and passed them to Caroline. Beatrix attempted to snatch them from her, but Edward put out a hand to stop her.

"It was an excellent idea of yours, Bea," he said wearily. "And it is a pity that it did not work out as you planned, although we came so near to success. We can never lay claim to a part of the estate now, notwithstanding the fact that April would certainly have wished me to have it, had she known—"

"Be quiet, you fool!" Beatrix shouted at him. "You must excuse us now, Lord Hannaford. Since you know this woman is not your granddaughter, but an imposter, Edward and I may as well take our leave of you and permit you to deal with her however you see fit to do."

"I think not, Madam. As I said, the French authorities wish to question you about the death of my granddaughter. You cannot believe that, knowing you are responsible for her death, I should be foolish enough to allow the pair of you to walk out of here, so that you can disappear. Alan, I believe you will find that Wilcox is in the hall, waiting for a word from me. Please ask him to summon several strong footmen and see that this pair is held for the authorities, whom I have already notified."

"With the greatest of pleasure, Uncle. But if you had this information already, it was not necessary for me to bring Mrs. Logan to see you, was it?"

"Not at all," the earl said. "I only hope you were not too greatly out of pocket in fetching her. Nor that your feelings were too greatly abraded by the time you spent in her company. And of course, her identification of Miss Kingston did serve to have them incriminate themselves further."

"Then I must suppose the trip was not in vain," Alan replied.

"Not at all. In fact, I shall reimburse you for what you paid out. Now, will you please remove this pair?"

"Immediately, Uncle—but I have just one question for you, Ainsworth. If you had managed to get Caroline away to the seashore or wherever you were intending to take her—and then her memory had returned, what were you planning to do about her?"

"We had not thought about that—or at least, I had not. But I am certain that Bea would have been able to think of something," Edward answered.

"As she did in the case of April Ainsworth?"

"No—that was something quite different; I should never—Bea became jealous—"

"Be quiet, you fool," Beatrix shouted again, but Alan nodded.

"You see how it is, Uncle. A little questioning and the man will collapse and tell everything he knows. I have no doubt he is telling us the truth now, and that it was this woman who killed the real April." Alan gestured towards Beatrix.

"Nor have I," Hannaford said grimly. "She appears to be quite capable of anything. But the man was April's husband, and certainly did nothing to have her killer apprehended. Therefore, he is an accomplice, and so is equally guilty of her death. See that they are taken away, Alan, with no more delay. I cannot bear to look at them again. I do not know what I might do."

Alan quickly obeyed and the guilty pair were taken to the cellar to be locked up until the men from the nearest magistrate arrived, and the story was told to them. Tightly manacled, they were led off, Beatrix screaming curses at the earl, Alan, and especially Caroline, until one of the men gagged her with his kerchief.

"Cannot have her speaking in that way before the lady, can we?" he said to Alan.

"No, we cannot." Alan matched his grin, thinking of the times the older woman must have mistreated Caroline—as she doubtless had also done with April. *Poor cousin April,* he thought, *to have fallen into the clutches of this pair, especially, of this vicious woman.* "With your permission, Uncle, I shall go along with these gentlemen and present your evidence to Sir William. Unless you would prefer to do so yourself."

"No—you go and tend to the matter, Alan. As I have said, I am weary of the sight of them. You may also notify my man in Paris, who will contact the French authorities to send for them. They are extremely anxious to have this pair in their hands, for I understand that April's death must have been an unpleasant one. It makes me happy when I recall they still employ the guillotine there for murderers." He smiled grimly at Edward's whimper of fear. Beatrix, of course, was unable to make a sound through her gag, but her expression was demoniacal.

Seeing her look, Alan grinned. "Then I was right when I told Mrs. Logan that no one would hang for this." Edward whimpered again and Beatrix, unable to use her hands, kicked at him savagely.

When the group had left the house, the earl's smile vanished. He sank into his chair and buried his face in his hands. It had been so cruel of them to revive his belief that his granddaughter was alive—only to have it shattered in this fashion.

Except for their scheming, he might have continued to think April had died in the epidemic; that would have been more merciful than the kind of death she must have received at Beatrix' hands. He supposed it was worth what he was suffering to know that her murderers would be punished, but that did nothing to lessen his grief.

Caroline was tempted to go to him and tell him how sorry she was for what had been done to him, but thought it best to leave him alone with his grief. After all, he had thought that she was his granddaughter, so any sight of her must be painful to him. There was no way she could take the other's place, now that everyone knew the truth.

She slipped out of the study without the earl's notice and took refuge in her room for the last time. Lucy was in tears, but was obeying her mistress' orders.

"But why should you go away now, Mrs.—I mean Miss Kingston? Now, when those two are gone and everything seems to have worked out so well?"

Caroline laughed shakily. "If you keep on in this way, Lucy, you will have me in tears, too. Now that I know who I am, I must leave—and as soon as possible; there is no choice for me."

"But can I not go with you?" Lucy asked.

"I will have no need for a maid—nor could I afford to employ one. I do not doubt you can be kept on here—and you would not wish to be separated from *your* Edward, would you?"

"Better that than to lose you," the maid said fiercely. "You have been so kind to me. I shall never find anyone like you, if you leave me. And if I am not with you, who will care for all your beautiful gowns?"

"I shall have no need for them, either. They are much too fine for me. Pack these only." Caroline had chosen two of the plainest ones. Even these, she told herself, were far too elaborate for a governess, but they must serve until she had found a new position and could purchase more suitable clothing. She could only hope that a prospective employer would not think she had stolen them, but that they had been given to her when she left her last place—which, in a way, would be the truth. "I shall need only one case," she warned. "The smallest one."

When everything was packed, she embraced the weeping Lucy, caught up her case and carried down to the earl's study. "What is this?" he demanded when he saw her.

"I came to ask, your lordship, if you might permit one of the coachmen to drive me to the closest stage stop. I fear I cannot afford to hire a post chaise."

"But—why should you go? You had no part in their crime, but were as much of a victim as we," the earl protested. "We know that now."

"No, but I shall always be a reminder of it. Besides, I have no place here. You have no need for a governess in your household," Caroline said.

"True enough—but you have been like a granddaughter; you brought happiness into the house once more, if only for a time. I cannot permit you to leave in this way."

"No, your lordship, I must go." How could she say to him that she could not bear to remain where she could see Alan, knowing that she was unworthy of him?

"I do not understand your reasons, but if you feel that you must . . . " He looked down at the single case she had set down by her feet. "Why only this?" he asked, indicating it. "Do you wish to have your other gowns sent after you?"

"No—like everything I have found in the past months, they are not for me. Such gowns are not fit for a governess, but for an earl's granddaughter."

"Or for an earl's niece?" Alan asked from the doorway. As she whirled to face him, he added, "An earl's niece—by marriage?"

"Please—" she begged, barely able to restrain her tears. "Do not jest about such things."

"Jest? About my feelings for you?" He strode to Caroline's side, grasping her arms with both hands. "Uncle—"

The earl, however, had moved to the window and was silently staring out across the lawn, apparently unconcerned with what was occurring behind him. Alan grinned, then drew Caroline into his arms.

"No—I must not," she protested.

"I had not intended to make my intentions known publicly until I had more opportunity to talk to you, although I do not doubt everyone suspects them. But if you are running away . . . " Alan said.

"You know that I must. I have no place—"

"Tell me that you do not love me, and I shall let you go."

"I—" Caroline could not lie about this, even to save him. "You know I am not worthy to belong to this family. A governess—"

"My love, until my cousin died and I was pitchforked into my present position, I was a captain in the army. Not a successful one, I fear, and it had taken me many years to rise so high. Never was I mentioned in dispatches or awarded a medal. I should never have reached a higher rank. Here, at least, I flatter myself that I can be of some use."

"Oh, you are. I have seen how you love this place," Caroline said.

"I do love it—but I should be willing to spend the Seasons in London, so that you could wear all your beautiful gowns, and as many more of them as you like."

"That was not the reason—"

His kiss silenced her protest. The earl continued to pretend that he knew nothing, but was smiling to himself.

"You will stay—with me?" Alan asked at last.

"I do not see that I can do otherwise. You know I love you," Caroline replied.

"Uncle—will you be willing to accept a niece in the place of a granddaughter?"

The old man turned to beam at the pair of them. "As the child says, I do not see that I can do otherwise."